THE GRAVE ROBBERS' CHRONICLES

VOL 2

Angry Sea, Hidden Sands

BY XU LEI
TRANSLATED BY
KATHY MOK

The Grave Robbers' Chronicles:
Angry Sea, Hidden Sands
By Xu Lei
Translated by Kathy Mok

Copyright©2011 ThingsAsian Press

Edited by Janet Brown and Michelle Wong
Illustrated by Neo Lok Sze Wong

For information regarding permissions, write to:
ThingsAsian Press
3230 Scott Street
San Francisco, California 94123 USA
www.thingsasianpress.com
Printed in China

ISBN-13: 978-1-934159-32-3
ISBN-10: 1-934159-32-8

TABLE OF CONTENTS

CHAPTER ONE

THE BRONZE FISH WITH SNAKE BROWS

The lid of the box slowly opened. Inside there was space only for an object no bigger than my thumb, and what the box contained was just about that size—a small bronze fish.

I held it in my hand. The fish looked very ordinary, but the workmanship was exquisite, particularly the brows of the fish, which had been crafted to look like snakes.

Uncle Three returned, blowtorch in hand. Startled to see that the box was open, he asked, "How the hell did you manage to do that?"

I told him about the password numbers and he frowned. "This is getting more and more confusing. Who were those foreigners anyway?" He picked up the bronze fish, and his face clouded over. "What? I have one of those—it's a Bronze Fish with Snake Brows!"

He took something from his pocket and handed it to me. I looked at it and saw it was also a dainty little bronze fish. It too was about the size of my thumb, its brows were shaped like snakes, and its workmanship was superb. Every last scale on its tiny body was fine and smooth. It had to have come from the same place as the one in the purple-enameled gold box.

The only flaw in this lovely little fish was that almost ingrained between its tiny scales were bits of white grit that looked like lime. I was certain I knew where this had been found but to be sure, I asked my uncle, "Is this an ocean treasure? Did you once rob an undersea tomb?"

Uncle Three nodded and I felt a stab of surprise. Ocean treasures were antiques dredged up from the sea, usually pieces of white and blue porcelain. It was much easier to find treasures in the ocean than on land, because they often lay exposed on the seabed. But because of the microscopic organisms that lived in the ocean, many of the pieces were coated with a layer of white ashlike dirt which was extremely difficult to remove and made them less valuable. And my uncle, I knew, wasn't interested in going after anything that wasn't extremely precious.

"Only once," my uncle replied, "and I wish I never had done it. If I only could go back in time and change that decision, I'd be happily married now to the only woman I've ever wanted as my wife, with children to care for me in my old age."

I'd heard quite a bit about my uncle's lost love—a splendid woman whom he met when they both were robbing a grave. Her name was Wen-Jin, a graceful and quiet woman from the north of China, an archaeology student who was so well mannered and lovely that nobody would ever guess how she made her living.

Wen-Jin and Uncle Three were an inseparable team for five years, both romantically and professionally. Then one day, Wen-Jin disappeared. All I knew was that there had been a fatal accident when she entered a grave.

1. THE BRONZE FISH WITH SNAKE BROWS

I was only a few years old when this happened but I can still remember Uncle Three sitting silently for a week or so, grieving and heartbroken, slowly returning to his ebullient self. Now that he had brought the subject up, I wanted to find out more of the story, but, reluctant to pry into my uncle's private memories, I only asked, "When Wen-Jin met her accident, was it at an undersea grave?"

Uncle Three sighed and said, "We were both so young. I knew some of her archaeology classmates who had a vague idea of what I did for a living. I didn't try to hide my grave robbing from them and we all got along quite well. When they talked about going to the island of Xisha in the South China Sea on an archaeological expedition to search for a shipwreck, I decided to go along too. I didn't know," he paused as if he didn't want to admit what he was about to say, "I didn't know that recovering undersea treasure was so dangerous."

Although Uncle Three was an inexperienced maritime grave robber, he was determined to accompany Wen-Jin on this adventure and he lied so convincingly about his mythical nautical experience that he was allowed to join the expedition.

The group of students rented two fishing boats and sailed to Xisha and the west side of the coral reefs. This was one of the most dangerous passages of the historical maritime Silk Road, where many ships had sunk. When Uncle Three dove down to have a look, he was stunned. Pieces of broken blue and white porcelain covered the ocean floor, strewn about when the ships sunk and broke into pieces.

The group dove underwater for several days and gathered basket after basket of broken porcelain. Uncle Three was good at identifying different types of porcelain; he was after all a grave robber. He could easily pick up a blue and white fragment and talk about it for half a day, and this made him the expedition's unofficial leader. The students called him Captain Wu Sensheng, and Uncle Three began to feel smug, self-important, and in command.

On the fourth day, one of the men kayaked far out into the sea and failed to return by nightfall. Worried, the group began to search and found his kayak on a reef about two kilometers away. Their friend was nowhere to be seen.

"Something went wrong," my uncle said. "Probably he dove down to explore on his own and had an accident." Grabbing his own diving equipment, Uncle Three plunged into the ocean to investigate.

Around midnight he found the missing man's body, one foot held fast in a crevice of the coral reef. He pulled the corpse to the water's surface and saw something clutched in the dead man's left hand. Prying the fingers open, my uncle found a small and intricately crafted tiny bronze fish with the brows of a snake.

While everyone grieved the death of their friend, Uncle Three decided there might be something valuable underwater where the corpse had been found. Perhaps while looking around with the rest of the group the day before, the dead man had seen something which he intended to keep for himself. Coming back alone as darkness fell, he had found death, not treasure, but the fish that he clutched in his dead fingers meant that he had found something valuable before he lost his life.

The next morning, Uncle Three gave an expurgated version of his scenario, being careful not to tarnish the dead man's reputation. "Our dead friend obviously worked overtime to benefit our team and he has paid for his dedication with his life," he announced to the group. "But it seems as though before he died, he found something precious. He exchanged his own life for the Bronze Fish with Snake Brows that we now have as proof of what might be a larger discovery, so we should carry on his efforts to honor his memory."

His speech encouraged the team to resume their expedition in spite of their sadness and they returned to the spot where they had found their friend's body. After thoroughly searching underwater, they found forty gigantic stone anchors lying on the seabed, all the same size and shape and carved with an ancient text that nobody could read.

Uncle Three speculated that these anchors could have come from forty missing boats that were all the same size or possibly were all from one large ship. Since it seemed implausible that forty identical boats could have all gone down at the same spot, he was sure there must be an enormous sunken ship somewhere in the area, so huge that it needed forty anchors to keep it immobile.

With his knowledge of history, my uncle felt he was qualified to make what might seem like a wild guess. When he and his team came back up to the ocean's surface, he muttered to Wen-Jin, "It looks like there's a tomb buried in this spot at the bottom of the sea."

CHAPTER TWO

THE DOUBLE-PANELED TOMB WALL

Uncle Three lay awake all that night. He had never robbed an undersea grave before but since he had lied so elaborately about his talent, somehow he had to back up his story in the morning.

A tomb in a sunken ship was basically a mausoleum built into the vessel; an undersea valley or trench was found in the ocean floor and there the ship was deliberately scuttled so the tomb would sink. Then it was sealed off and covered with a layer of heavy soil. It was identical to a burial site on dry land but was so difficult to accomplish that legend said only one person had been buried this way—the son of the fabulously wealthy Shen Manzo.

When a burial ship sank, there had to be a lot of anchors attached to it so it wouldn't drift to another spot. So my uncle calculated that the center at which the anchors were dropped, or a spot deviating slightly from that point, would definitely mark the burial site.

The next day Uncle Three took his crew underwater and linked all the anchors together with ropes. Then he placed a marker in the middle of the confined area and told his group to plunge their shovels into various spots around that point. As he had hoped, they discovered a piece of wood close to the east side of the center.

Using his traditional positioning technique, my uncle found a gigantic underground palace in the T shape of the Chinese character for "soil." The palace was made up of two ear chambers, two rooms of identical size and shape, and a hall in the back of the structure. This was the largest space of all and seemed to be the spot where the coffin would be.

Uncle Three was amazed—who could be buried in such an intricately constructed tomb, which was as large as the burial grounds of an emperor? Everyone was so excited they stayed up all that night, discussing how they would enter the tomb.

After hours of discussion, the team decided how they would work their way through the ocean floor. The fishermen kept dynamite aboard to kill large groups of fish. Using this, Uncle Three and his crew would blast away the sand on top of the burial site and then dig a slanted tunnel through the stabler soil found below the treacherous sand.

This was an enormous job that my uncle estimated would take about a week to accomplish, but the crew was eager to begin the task. However, there was an immediate problem to solve. The corpse of their dead comrade needed to be taken back to shore before it began to stink.

They all agreed that the larger of their two boats would carry the body back to land while the

2. THE DOUBLE-PANELED TOMB WALL

excavation team would use the smaller one as a base. The weather was good, the sea was calm, they had no need to worry. Tying three kayaks together, they moved all of the equipment they would need onto the rocks of the reef.

Once the bigger boat sailed off, Uncle Three realized they had lost the backup provided by an extra vessel and felt a twinge of apprehension. But the excitement of uncovering the gigantic tomb and all that it contained soon chased away any worry. The group dug the tunnel much more rapidly than he had anticipated and they reached the walls of the tomb after only four days.

The big boat had still not returned and the crew began to wonder what had delayed it. Only hard work kept them from panic and Uncle Three urged them on with stories of the treasure that waited for them within the tomb. They quickly dismantled part of the wall, revealing a dark emptiness within.

Uncle Three told his crew to stop digging, turned on his flashlight, and climbed in through the opening alone. There was another wall.

Crouched between the inner and outer barriers, he looked around and saw above his head a small opening that led to an inner chamber. Suddenly he knew that digging alone wouldn't be enough to allow entry to this tomb.

Ordering the crew to rise back up to the reef, Uncle Three told them, "There are two walls in this tomb with water filling the area between the inner and the outer walls. There's a tunnel through the inner wall where the water spirals inward. This means that there must be a dry area inside that uses air pressure to leave a portion of oxygen inside the chamber. Right now I don't know how long the tunnel is. Three of us will go down tomorrow. Each one of us will bring four respirators and we'll see if we can get to the tunnel's end."

His speech was stopped by Wen-Jin's scream. The reef they were on had risen into the air and they were now high above the water. My uncle looked at the sky and saw a black line approaching from the horizon.

One of the students, Li Sidi, was a fisherman's son. His voice quavered, "Oh shit, a huge storm is on its way."

CHAPTER THREE
THE STORM

"Look at how the sea has receded," Li Sidi told his companions. "In a couple of minutes, the water that has been sucked away will come charging back in a tsunami. Since we have only three small kayaks to carry us to safety, we're in trouble now."

"We're going to die," one of the students muttered, and some of the girls began to sob hysterically. Uncle Three took Wen-Jin's hand. Her palm was sweating, and he knew that, although she was silent, she was as frightened as the girls who wept.

Uncle Three had never been in this situation before but he was a professional grave robber; his nervous system was impervious to stress. He knew he didn't have the luxury of becoming upset. If his mind was clouded by emotion, then all of them were sure to die.

He did a head count. There had been ten in their group when they embarked on this adventure, but one had died and another had taken the corpse to shore. Now there were eight.

"How long will this storm last?" my uncle asked Li Sidi.

"These monsoon storms last a very short time; it should be over in about ten minutes. But during that time, the

sea will rise to the point that our reef will be completely submerged." Li Sidi shook his head. "It may only last ten minutes but each second will be deadly. The coming tsunami will be smaller than normal but even so, it will dash us against the rocks of the reef or sweep us out to sea."

Uncle Three's mind searched quickly for solutions. To take the kayaks back to their boat now would be suicidal; they could never outrun the storm no matter how fast they rowed. And the surrounding waters weren't deep enough for them to hide beneath the sea's surface and breathe through their respirators.

Uncle Three looked into the sea; he could almost see the bottom clearly. As if a flash of lightning had shot through the dark night, a very risky plan leaped into his mind. He had no time to mull it over for flaws. "We can't think too much now," he blurted. "Gather up the respirators and let's see how much oxygen we have left. Then we'll go down to the undersea tomb to take shelter from the storm."

Going into ancient tombs was something Uncle Three had done so often that for him it was like walking into his own house, but this wasn't the case for most of his scholarly crew. Murmurs of shock and doubt began to fill the air, and my uncle realized he had presented his solution too bluntly.

Speaking quickly and emphatically, he pointed at the coming storm. "Look at this. It's not upon us yet but we know what to expect. We've all seen TV footage about tsunamis. If we sit here and wait, we'll have no chance of staying alive and our bodies will never be found. Under the water's surface is a ready-made shelter. We already know that there's air inside. There are only a few of us so there will be enough oxygen to keep everyone alive. We can wait in the tomb for an hour and then come back out. This is our only chance."

Uncle Three had a natural talent for persuasion and it worked for him now. Everyone felt a glimmer of hope as they gathered their diving equipment. Quickly showing the group a few gestures of sign language to use underwater, my uncle led them down to the bottom of the sea. He turned on a waterproof flashlight, and was the first to crawl into the grave tunnel.

In those days divers wore huge helmets that looked absurd but were very durable and protective. No sea creature, no matter how large, could swallow up anyone who wore this diving helmet, Uncle Three reminded himself, and tried to relax as he swam.

The walls of the tomb were covered with carvings of human faces, which fascinated the group so much that they forgot the danger they were in and crowded together to examine them. Uncle Three urged them to keep moving if they wanted to save themselves—he could feel a headache coming on.

They all swam onward for about fifteen minutes, took a few turns, and lost their sense of direction. They were all becoming disoriented and my uncle realized he had to pull them together. Signaling everyone to stop, he asked Wen-Jin to do a headcount to make sure that no one had been left behind.

Exhausted from swimming in the narrow tunnel, the students all collapsed on the floor when they saw the signal to stop as if they were kindergarten children ready for their naps. Being the captain really sucks, my uncle thought. He pointed his flashlight toward the others just as Wen-Jin tapped his leg. She looked frightened and Uncle Three thought oh hell, is someone missing?

Wen-Jin looked confused, as if she no longer knew how to express herself. She pointed a finger and waved it nonstop in front of Uncle Three's face. Not understanding her, he asked her if one person was missing. Wen-Jin read his lips, shook her head, pointed up all fingers on one hand, and then four fingers on the other. Then she put her two hands together. Suddenly Uncle Three understood— she was trying to tell him, "There should only be eight of us but now there are nine."

CHAPTER FOUR
THE SEA GHOST

Uncle Three was horrified. He could understand if one or two people were missing. It would even make sense if everyone had disappeared. But for an extra person to appear out of thin air was unbelievable. Perhaps Wen-Jin had made a mistake, he thought, and turned around to count the group. He began with himself first, Wen-Jin second, and he went on in order, the third, the fourth, the fifth, the sixth, the seventh, the eighth was Li Sidi, and the...

Suddenly he choked. He could see the ninth person hiding in the back of the group, looking blurry and indistinct; he began to sweat. My uncle wasn't afraid of ghosts or zombies, but he had no idea what lurked beneath the surface of the sea. Did zombies know how to swim? Was there any such thing as a sea zombie?

He shook his head and began to blame Li Sidi for being so goddamn mindless, slow, and unable to notice that something was following him from behind. He could count on nobody but himself. Finding a knife in his tool bag, he hid it under his arm and swam over to the ninth man, who stood motionless.

Li Sidi saw Uncle Three charging in his direction and realized something was behind him. He turned his head to look, but as he moved, the ninth man also moved, as if in imitation. Alarmed, Li Sidi took a few steps back. The ninth man also took a few steps back.

This isn't just strange, it's ridiculous, my uncle decided and pointed his flashlight at the ninth man. Startled by the light, the stranger scurried backward in an attempt to escape, and my uncle saw a savage, monstrous face covered with scales.

In a panic Li Sidi looked at Uncle Three, his mouth stretched in a scream that was silent beneath his helmet. Realizing he was hysterical, my uncle removed his helmet and slapped him. Li Sidi fell back against the wall of the tunnel and it buckled beneath his weight. The water gushed through it like a flooding river and Uncle Three and his companions were sucked through the wall like cockroaches in a toilet.

My uncle had no idea how many times he was whirled around and around. He felt as if his heart, lungs, and liver had all been shoved over to the left side of his body. His head struck something but his helmet protected him. Looking up, he saw he was in a chamber, no longer in the water, and his companions were with him. He grabbed Wen-Jin in a tight embrace, and then looked at their surroundings. They were within the tomb.

Uncle Three reached into a zippered pocket of his wet suit and took out a waterproof lighter. It ignited, which proved the room had oxygen. He took off his helmet and his companions followed his example. There was a pleasant aroma in the chamber, a light fragrance that was very refreshing. "Where does that scent come from?" Wen-Jin asked and my uncle shrugged, "I've been in a lot of tombs that stunk but never found one that smelled this nice—damned if I know."

He swept the room with a small flashlight that had been safely zipped inside his pocket. The room, he decided, had to be one of the ear chambers, since it held no coffin. Piles of porcelain lay on the floor, perhaps used by the tomb's occupant before he died. In the center of the room was a circular opening which seemed to lead outward.

On the wall, murals had been painted which had deteriorated over the centuries; the shadowy figures pictured within them had human shapes—tall, short, fat, walking, dancing. Each was drawn realistically as if it had been photocopied—with one strange feature. All of their stomachs were very large, as if the figures were all pregnant.

Although Wen-Jin had studied the art of ancient murals, she was as puzzled by these figures as my uncle was, but Li Sidi began to shriek. "Sea ghosts—this is a grave for sea ghosts!"

Uncle Three thought of the monster they had just encountered a while ago. Could it have been a sea ghost? He knew it would only lead to panic if he raised the possibility so he decided to keep this thought to himself.

Looking at the group, he saw some of them had already begun to walk toward the door of the ear chamber. "Stop," he warned them. "We don't have any excavation equipment now, or first aid supplies. Wait here, all of you. We don't know if there are any traps in this tomb. We're seeking refuge, so everyone must be grateful and patient."

4. THE SEA GHOST

Although reluctant to obey, the students began to examine the burial porcelain. Uncle Three knew at first glance these came from the early Ming dynasty. Shit, he wondered, could this really be the burial site of Shen Manzo's son?

But he had seen many antiques in his work and had no interest in these. At the moment, he was more concerned whether there was enough air for all in this space. He checked the number of the people again; once again there were only eight and as he allowed himself to feel relieved, he realized how exhausted he was. He began to yawn; the lovely aroma in the air seemed to have a tranquilizing effect. Suddenly he felt unable to keep his lids from drooping and told Wen-Jin, "I'm going to sleep for a while. Wake me in an hour or so."

Hazily he wondered if the fragrance that filled his nostrils was from something in the tomb or from the sweetness of Wen-Jin's hair, but before he could decide, he was sound asleep.

CHAPTER FIVE
AN OLD SNAPSHOT

As I listened to this story, I could feel myself in that ancient tomb with Wen-Jin in my arms. Uncle Three coughed and I returned to the present, embarrassed to find myself hugging a pillow. Hell, I was fantasizing about Uncle Three's dead woman. Turning scarlet, I asked, "Why did you stop? What happened next?"

Uncle Three smiled sadly. "There's nothing else to say; that's the end of the story. I still can't figure out what happened in that damn tomb while I slept." His voice shook as he spoke. "I don't know how long I slept. When I woke up, I was the only person left in that chamber. Everyone else was gone. I thought they went to the main tomb and I was furious. Wen-Jin always listened to me, and I couldn't believe she had gone off with the others. I got up ready to chase after them."

He put down a cigarette that had been between his lips. Looking a bit awkward, he continued, "Then I turned to the door on the wall and found that it was gone! I turned around and discovered at once that this was not the ear chamber where I had fallen asleep. This was a strange place; behind me was a gold coffin made of nanmu wood—you know, the rarest kind that doesn't rot and can last for over two thousand years."

I laughed. "Uncle Three, as daring and determined as you are, I'm sure you didn't think twice before opening the coffin and pouring out every treasure it contained."

"Fuck you—I was so scared I almost pissed myself. I've seen a lot of coffins in my life, but there was water coming nonstop out of that one. It was like some goddamn thing was taking a bath in there. Then I remembered Li Sidi said this was a tomb of sea ghosts. That had me really ready to wet my pants, and at the same time I was worried about Wen-Jin. I shouted a few more times but there was no answer. And then the coffin lid opened all by itself.

"I didn't even think twice. I took one look at the helmet in my hand and put it on. Then I jumped right into the circular opening in the middle of the room and got the hell out of there."

"Oh come off it," I objected, "I thought you woke up in a different room from the one you fell asleep in? How come there was still a circular opening for you to leap into?"

Uncle Three began to stammer, "It was there. Of course it was. Don't interrupt me, goddamn it. I haven't finished yet!" He refocused and continued, "I didn't even care if there was a tsunami or not. When I found the opening of the cave, I swam out. The first thing I saw was a huge egg-yolk of a sun hanging in the sky and a few boats not far off that looked like they were coming to rescue us. I swam toward them and when they picked me up, I found out it was afternoon the next day. Hell! I only took a short nap in the tomb. How could a day have gone by just like that?"

As I stared at my uncle, I felt sure he was lying to me.

He had definitely come across something important in the end, and he wasn't telling me what it was. What the hell did the old bastard do in that tomb at the end? Damn it! I knew I couldn't force it out of him but the more evasive and suspicious he became, the more he left me itching to know more.

As he stopped speaking, I thought about Wen-Jin. "What about the others? Didn't they come out too?"

Uncle Three looked sick. "I got on the boat and after saying a few words, I fainted. I was sent to a hospital where I was in a coma for a week. When I wanted to go back and look for the others, I could no longer find the boatman who had taken us there. At sea, if you don't have the exact coordinates of a place, you'll never find it. The ocean looks exactly the same in all four directions." He paused and went on. "Then I went to the Maritime Administration as well as to the research institute, and found that the whole group had been reported as missing—Wen-Jin too. It's been almost twenty years, and I still don't know what happened in that tomb. How could people go missing for no reason?" Red-eyed, he slapped the table angrily. "Fuck it. I really regret this. Why the hell did I have to show off? If I didn't try to rob that undersea grave, everybody on our team would probably have grandkids by now! And then—Wen-Jin, shit I am sorry about her. I'll always miss her."

Uncle Three was teary-eyed and snorting loudly. I'd never seen him like this before, and I didn't know what to do. Holding up the Bronze Fish with Snake Brows, he said, "In the end, I thought about it for a long time. I wondered why I was the only one who got out while none of the others did. The only difference between me and them was that I carried this with me."

I looked at the fish and said, "Perhaps our Ruler of Dead Soldiers robbed an undersea grave too, since he also carried a Bronze Fish with Snake Brows. Could there be some connection between the tomb of the Rulers and that in the sunken ship?" However, this was absolutely impossible. The construction of these two tombs was separated by a long period of time. One was built during the Warring States Period, while the other was built in the early Ming dynasty. It was preposterous to draw any connection between them.

But Uncle Three wasn't listening to me; he was lying on his bed, looking thoughtful. Suddenly he sat up and said, "Nephew, I just remembered something."

He turned so pale that I knew he must have thought of something terrible. He shook his head and said, "One of the students that went into the undersea tomb looked a lot like Poker-face!"

My scalp felt numb when I heard what he said. "You're out of your goddamn mind. He was only a baby when that happened."

Uncle Three frowned and his eyebrows puckered more and more. Finally he said, "It's such a long time ago. I can't be sure. But I still have the group photo from that time. It was taken right before we set out. Let me get a scan from home."

He made a phone call and five minutes later an e-mail appeared on his cell phone. He opened it and showed me the picture that was attached.

It was an old black-and-white photo of ten people separated into two rows, with the front row squatting and the back row standing. I could see that the middle one in the squatting row was Uncle Three and the guy standing behind him was indubitably Poker-face. Impossible, I thought, and blinked hard to clear my sight. But when I looked again it was still him. His eyes and his face were exactly the same as he looked when I saw him a week or two ago, twenty years after this picture had been taken.

Uncle Three glanced over at me. He was unable to get his words out for a long time, as if something was stuck in his throat. Finally he asked, "Why...why didn't he get any older after two decades?" Then he looked wide awake, shouting like a crazy man, "Oh, now I get it!"

He grabbed his suitcase and began to walk out the door. I pulled at him but he flung me away, saying, "You wait here for Panzi to get well. I have to go to Xisha right now." Turning away, he ran from me without looking back.

CHAPTER SIX
FORBIDDEN LADY

"What the hell are you doing?" I yelled, but all I heard was the word "Elevator" as my uncle ran down the hallway. He almost collided with the hotel manager who was approaching our room, bill in hand.

"So your uncle's left you to take care of his foot massages, has he? He's been quite a devoted customer." The manager smiled. I did my best to match his good humor, but my smile turned into a grimace when I saw that the bill he handed me was for more than four thousand yuan.

I was pissed off. Uncle Three often proclaimed that he was too old-fashioned to use credit cards when he traveled. He had run out of cash after we took Panzi to the hospital and had been using my money ever since, assuring me he'd reimburse me when his company sent him more funds. I wondered if this massive massage bill was the reason he had fled the scene. I felt very bitter, and then as I took out my wallet, sick enough to puke. I'd been too busy forking over money to notice what I had left. It wasn't very much.

Panzi was still in a coma, alone and helpless, with nobody but me to take care of him. Although his doctor

said there was nothing seriously wrong with him and that his body was just taking the time it needed to heal, I knew it would probably be another week before he came back to the world, and meanwhile his hospital bill came to one thousand yuan a day. The miserable amount of cash in my wallet wasn't going to be enough for him—let alone the money my uncle had racked up with the hotel's massage girls.

I managed to pull off a sickly smile. "I don't have enough cash with me at the moment. It will take a minute or two for me to get what I owe you." Since the manager had noticed how prodigally my uncle and I had spent our money recently, he assured me, "That's okay—don't worry. Do what you need to do. You can settle this tomorrow."

Once he left, I began to panic. How the fuck was I going to come up with this money? My uncle was God-knows-where and I certainly couldn't ask my father. I could well imagine what he'd have to say: "First you let your business go to hell and then you abandon everything to follow your grave-robbing uncle—forget it. I'm not giving you one yuan."

As I stared wild-eyed around the hotel room, in the corner I saw the one treasure we brought out of the tomb of the Ruler of Dead Soldiers—the jade coffin cover that my uncle had been so careful to bring out in one piece. Uncle Three and I had talked about what we could get for this treasure; he'd said it was easily worth one million yuan and he'd never let it go for less than eight hundred grand. That sounded good to me. It was time to find the local antique market and get some cash.

"Take me to the market that has the most antique dealers," I told a taxi driver and once I arrived, I began to look for the largest shop since it would have well-established customers. I took only a few steps when I saw in a shop window a bronze incense burner engraved with the same swollen-bellied figures that Uncle Three had seen in the murals of the undersea tomb. I stooped down to look more closely when the shop owner came out and remarked, "You're a man who can tell the good from the bad; that's the only valuable piece in my shop."

I could tell from his accent that this guy was from Beijing and was probably sharper than most of his competitors so I played dumb. "What's carved on that? It's so weird. That's not from Hainan, is it?"

He grabbed my sleeve and pulled me inside his shop. "At last, an expert! I've had this piece for years and you're the first man to notice it. Yes, this is from the coast, from Hainan."

Flattery was part of the antique trade; I had no idea if this guy was telling me the truth or lying to make a sale. "I'm no expert," I replied, "I just saw something like this when I was in Hainan and thought it was weird. I don't even know what it is."

"Come, sit down and have a cup of tea with me. I'll tell you—the figures carved on this incense burner represent a ghost called the Forbidden Lady and she has a long story. Do you want to hear it?"

I nodded eagerly and he laughed as he put the burner on a table nearby. A strange aroma wafted from it and I asked, "What is that smell?"

6. FORBIDDEN LADY

He opened the lid of the burner; inside were many small black objects that looked like pebbles. "These are the Forbidden Lady's bones. The smell that comes from them is called the bone fragrance and it's good stuff. I guarantee you'll have a sweet and comfortable sleep if you light this and put it beside your bed."

Suddenly I felt a little sick and asked, "Who the hell is this Forbidden Lady anyway? It would be disgusting to go to sleep smelling her bones."

"Ah, the Forbidden Lady is evil incarnate. Anyone who is ill or injured has been touched by the Forbidden Lady. It's difficult to describe what she really is but if I have to try, I guess I'd say she's a devil."

"Ah—so these are her bones?" I frowned and asked, "Where did this come from? Judging by the dirt on the lid, it looks like it was found under the sea, right?"

The man chuckled and said, "And you say you're not an expert! That's right. This was brought up by a fisherman's net. But when a thing is rare, it is precious. Although there's some sea dirt on this, the price is still pretty high."

I sighed, "Unfortunately, I prefer clean objects. I don't want this item from the sea. If you really want to make a sale, why not sell me the bits of bone inside it?"

The man's face clouded but he clapped on another smile. "How could I do that? If you buy the bones, who will ever want the incense burner?"

No wonder he was pushing it so heavily—it was very dusty and obviously had been in the window for a long time. I knew once I showed this guy the jade coffin cover, he'd give me this and anything else in his shop that I might show an interest in. I shook my head and smiled,

"That's okay. Forget it. I have something to show you."

I opened my bag and showed him a corner of the cover; his reaction would tell me if this guy was an expert. His face turned solemn and he carefully tucked the jade back into the bag without saying a word. Then he closed the shutters of the shop, dumped out the tea he had poured for me, and replaced it with another cup. From its fragrance, I knew he was giving me the finest oolong. I'd come to the right place.

The shopkeeper cleared his throat and asked, "How may I address you, sir?"

He was no half-wit; he knew at one glance that this was something robbed from a grave. So I smiled politely. "My last name is Wu. What may I call you, master?"

"You can call me Lao Hai," he responded. "So, Master Wu. Do you want to sell this or are you just letting me peek at it for fun?"

I said, "Of course I'm selling. This thing is a bit uncomfortable to hold onto; it scorches my fingers."

"Is it all in one piece?"

I nodded. "Not one link is broken. It's just out of the pot. Still warm."

He sat down and said softly, "Well, Master Wu, I daresay that I am the only person in this entire market who would take this. It's unnecessary to haggle; treasures like this can't be bargained for like a bag of potatoes. Why don't you give me an honest price, and I'll call a friend and ask if he'll buy it."

I thought for a moment. I knew from my uncle that this was worth at least one million yuan. Big Kui's family would receive three hundred grand. Panzi's medical expenses would rise to two hundred grand at least. Fats had left a message earlier saying if we sold this, we should wire him his share of the proceeds. There went another hundred grand or more.

When I thought about how we all had gambled our lives for this—and Big Kui losing his—I felt one million was too little, but Uncle Three had told me that was the harsh reality of grave robbing and why we kept going from one grave to the next. No matter how precious an object might be, it was still rubbish if no one wanted to buy it. Therefore, he would not even take valuable things when he was in a grave if he knew they could not be sold.

I estimated that one million would do, so I gestured that figure to Lao Hai. He was delighted, and I felt slightly stupid when I saw his reaction. Was my price too low? He picked up his phone, huddled in a corner, and whispered for a while. When he returned, he was so overjoyed that his face looked like a ripe apple.

"It's done! It's done! Master Wu, you're in luck! I asked for 1.2 million for you. What do you think about that?"

How the hell did I know how much he'd really asked for? He could well have asked his client for double that price. But since it was already two hundred grand more than I had expected, I was happy enough.

I smiled. "So should we calculate your share in the customary manner?"

He beamed and said, "I won't hide the truth from you. The other side has already offered me something; you can keep the entire 1.2 million. Next time you have stuff like this, just come to me right away and I'll raise whatever price you ask by twenty percent. My most important customer is a rich man who collects things that others can't afford."

He saw that I looked a bit impatient and quickly reassured me. "Why don't you sit here for a while? I'll go and get the money for you. Don't judge my shop by its looks. Although it's small, my account has ample assets. I'll advance the 1.2 million for you."

"Hold on! What about this Forbidden Lady incense burner? If you give me a discount I'll take the whole thing," I blurted before he walked out the door.

Laughing and waving his hand, he said, "Oh that—if you like it, take it. I got it for five yuan. I was just bullshitting you with all that crap about the bone fragrance."

Three hours later, I was carrying a tidy sum of cash with a smile on my face that was so big nobody could see my eyes.

I paid all the hotel bills and handed over a month's worth of Panzi's medical costs to the hospital. I sent Fats his share and I transferred my share, plus what Uncle Three owed me, to my account. Life was good.

I found a pretty tour guide to show me around but the more scenery I saw, the less I gave a damn about any of it. All I wanted was to find a place to go fishing. But leisure and relaxation brought out the despicable side of my character—I actually began to miss grave robbing.

I came back to my room one day and heard the phone ringing the minute I walked in the door. Only Uncle Three knew the phone number of our hotel room, so I knew he had to be calling to finally let me know why he had rushed off like a crazy person. Instead there was a voice I'd never heard before who asked without any kind of pleasantries, "Do you know a guy named Wu Sansheng?"

"Yes, I know him," I replied. "What's the problem?"

"He's missing," the man on the phone told me.

"What do you mean, missing?"

"We've had no contact with his boat for the past ten days. What's your relationship to him?"

I replied, "I'm his nephew."

"Then please come to Hainan right away."

CHAPTER SEVEN
MEETING MISS NING

It turned out the guy who called me worked for a large international company that specialized in "marine resource development," or undersea grave robbing that was professional and legitimate. Using historical and archaeological consultants, it located ancient shipwrecks and salvaged the sunken cargo to sell to museums or collectors. It was a successful and profitable enterprise, and Uncle Three turned to them to rent a boat and equipment after he had fled the hotel.

Leasing what he needed from this business and recruiting a five-man crew under the company's name, my uncle had maintained radio contact for five days—and then he and the boat vanished. Three hours before the boat dissolved into thin air, Uncle Three had reported that he had found the underwater tomb he had been seeking and that he along with three of the crew were preparing to dive down and enter it.

The company waited for forty-eight hours before sending out a search party, which found not a trace of their boat nor the man who had rented it from them. Uncle Three had given them my phone number before he left as an emergency contact, and they decided this was indeed an emergency.

The man on the phone now told me, "We have no idea of what happened in this tomb, nor do we know where it is nor if your uncle and his men are still alive, so we're organizing another team to go in and get some answers. Because most of us plan explorations rather than embark upon them, we need an experienced guide to help our team pinpoint the exact location of the tomb and we think you're the man for the job."

"We can talk about this when we meet," I responded and the voice said, "The sooner the better."

I hung up, packed rapidly, and asked the desk clerk to reserve a ticket for the next available flight to Hainan. For ten hours I moved nonstop, with no time to imagine what had happened to my uncle but hoping that the old pain in the ass was still alive. When my flight landed, a car was waiting for me and the driver told me that the company was very concerned about my uncle's disappearance because one of his crew was the son of a highly placed executive. Since the incident took place in the waters of the politically contentious South China Sea, it could not be made public so it was necessary to use only people who had no government connections.

When we arrived at the pier, a middle-aged man came up and asked, "Are you Mr. Wu?"

I nodded, and he opened the car door for me. "Please follow me. Our boat is about to leave."

"Boat," I asked, "what boat? Leaving for where? Aren't you taking me to a hotel?"

Shaking his head, he replied, "No time for that—we have seven hours to reach the spot where we lost contact with your uncle, and we must wind this mission up ten hours after that. Otherwise, we face a two-week monsoon period, when we can offer no support for those who are lost. This is a real mess your uncle has stuck us with."

I was a little pissed off that I had no time to shower or rest before going to work but with my uncle's life at stake, all I could do was mumble okay and fall into line. The man pointed to an extremely ramshackle boat anchored nearby and said, "Here you are—it's all ready for your expedition."

I was sure he was joking but he continued, "We have no choice. The border patrol is already suspicious about our activity and we need to keep a low profile. But don't worry—we have sophisticated equipment on this tub and you'll have no problem doing what you need to do."

He took my hand, shook it, and said, "Miss Ning is the coordinator of this expedition. She's right here, just behind you. Good luck!"

His efficiency and sheer gall had me flabbergasted. I'd landed less than an hour ago and this guy had already walked away, leaving me on a crappy-looking boat. I turned to see a young woman in a very sexy, form-fitting wet suit who laughed at my bewildered face. She beckoned and said, "Come on. I'll show you what you're in for."

CHAPTER EIGHT
IN TROUBLE

I followed Ning into the cabin, which was crammed with diving equipment, tools, ropes, and boxes of food. It was difficult to find space to walk through the jumble of cartons, which looked as though they had been thrown on board with no organization—a bad sign, I thought.

There were a few bunks in a small space behind the engine room. They were covered with bedding that already reeked of motor oil; sitting on one of them was a stout, bald, middle-aged man. He stood up as I approached him and shook my hand, saying, "What a pleasure to meet a colleague. Welcome aboard. My humble name is Zhang."

His stilted courtesy put me off immediately but out of politeness, I returned his handshake. To my surprise, his grip was tight and firm. His hand felt rough, as though he had done more than his share of manual labor, in an odd contrast to his smooth-skinned baby face.

Ning introduced us. "Mr. Zhang is a consultant especially invited by our company to lend his knowledge to our expedition. He is an expert in underwater palaces of the Ming dynasty and will be in charge of analyzing the grave that we seek."

Archaeology didn't interest me very much and neither did Baldy, which I decided would be my private name for this guy. But seeing that he was pleased with Ning's introduction, I said, "I have been looking forward to meeting you."

Baldy waved his hand and announced pompously, "Oh please, I don't deserve to be called an expert, only a researcher who has had more luck than others. I happen to have published several papers in academic journals, small achievements that aren't worth mentioning."

Is this man serious, I wondered and rejected several sarcastic responses that immediately popped into my head. "You are far too humble," I remarked, trying not to laugh.

He took me seriously, of course, and pumped my hand again as he asked, "May I know on what basis Mr. Wu was invited on this expedition? Forgive me for being blunt, but it seems, Mr. Wu, that your research subject is a bit obscure. Perhaps I am ignorant and ill-informed but I have never come across Mr. Wu's name in any archaeological magazine."

His words and his tone of voice were both condescending, and it was hard to tell if that was intentional. Short-tempered from worry and weariness, I almost blew up. But I'd been on board for just a few minutes and needed to see how things stood here, so I swallowed my annoyance and only said, "I'm an excavation specialist."

I hoped my terse reply would shut him up, but he was unconcerned with anybody's words except his own. "Oh, you must be an architect? No wonder I've never heard of you," he babbled. "We come from such different disciplines! But we can certainly be considered professional half brothers. You build houses for a living, and I study the houses of the dead. We have something in common."

I did not know whether to laugh or walk away. He was so over the top, it seemed as though he had to be joking but he looked dead serious. I tried to match his solemn and pedantic manner as I replied, "But I'm no architect. I'm an excavator. Before you are able to study the houses of the dead, first I have to dig them up for you."

I regretted these words the minute I said them, since I hadn't yet decided whether I would go down into the tomb myself, nor would I until I found out what was going on here. I added quickly, "But whether we'll dig or not depends on what we find when we reach the tomb. It will be impossible to excavate if the conditions aren't right."

"Oh, of course, Mr. Wu, of course. Here, please do me the honor of accepting my business card. The more friends we have, the more pathways open up before us. If you ever come to the north, I will always be happy to help you in any way I can." This bald jerk was unbelievable—I'd only met him a few minutes ago and he already behaved as if we'd been friends for ten years. If I kept talking to him for another five minutes, he'd probably be certain I was his long-lost brother, so I hastily turned to Ning and asked her to tell me all she knew about my uncle's disappearance.

"It seems that when your uncle set off on his expedition, he was unsure of the exact location of this undersea tomb so he identified four possible sites and went to each one in turn. The last place he went had to have been the site they were looking for, but his final communication was brief and gave no indication of where they were. So now we'll have to go to each of the four sites, spending only half an hour at each spot.

"We're lucky that the sea is so calm and clear. With the sun as strong as it is, we can see all the way to the bottom. The water flowing over the seabed is smooth, stirring up very little sand, so anything that your uncle uncovered a few days ago should still be visible.

"I'm sure your uncle and his men are still alive, Mr, Wu, please don't be too worried," Ning concluded and although I had no idea why she felt this way, I was grateful for her optimism and hoped I'd find it was contagious.

Since Baldy hadn't been included in this conversation, he returned to his bunk, probably in a snit. Although he was obviously middle-aged, he had the temperament of a spoiled child and would no doubt be that way if he lived to be one hundred. Getting along with this jerk over the next few days is going to be a challenge, I thought gloomily.

The engine roared into life, the captain raised the anchor, and we were off to sea. The boat immediately began rocking violently, sideways and back and forth. I was exhausted from my long flight by traveling for more than ten hours and the boat's cradle-like rocking nourished my fatigue. I yawned, Ning suggested I take a nap, and without hesitation I collapsed onto one of the hard bunks and fell asleep.

When I woke up, there was no land to be seen and the surrounding water was like a slab of dark green jade. The sun had disappeared behind clumps of thick black clouds. A few shafts of light shone through gaps in the darkness,

8. IN TROUBLE

making a golden block print in the sky. The sun's beams were reflected in gleaming flecks that sparkled over the waves, but this beauty didn't last long.

Soon the dark clouds blended into one and devoured all the light; the ocean became hideously black and tossed our boat about like a nutshell. When we sank into the troughs of the waves, it looked as though the ocean was going to swallow us up.

The crew was busy racing back and forth to tighten the ropes that kept our supplies in place. I noticed that the captain showed no signs of consternation or fear and this was reassuring.

I was a city boy, accustomed to life on dry land, so this was more thrilling than frightening to me. I went up to the deck to lend a hand but rapidly discovered this wasn't as easy a task as I had imagined. It wasn't enough to just be able to react quickly in order to keep my footing—I had to be aware of the motion of the waves and the boat so I could guess after one tilt where the next would be and then prepare for it. Obviously this skill would take time to master; meanwhile after a few seconds I had to grab and hold onto something solid.

Some of the crew caught sight of something in the distance and began to yell words I couldn't understand. When I looked to see what they were pointing at, I made out a vague shape behind the waves to our left.

Ning came up behind me and I asked her to translate what the crew was shouting about. "They see a boat," she said.

The captain walked over and said in broken Mandarin, "It looks like another boat's had an accident over there.

According to the laws of the sea, we must go over and see if we can help."

Of course we made no objection. The captain quickly issued a string of commands and our boat veered to the left.

The sea was now its own universe and each wave was a mountain. Each time we passed through one, we plunged into a valley of water and were soaked through to the bone God knows how many times. I felt a weird exhilaration and shouted with excitement.

Our boat hurtled over several dozen waves before we finally could see a dim outline of the object ahead. I heard the captain bellow something that sounded like a curse and the crew began to run in a panic. I asked Miss Ning what was wrong and she seized my hand.

"Run and whatever you do, don't look back. That boat is full of sea ghosts!"

8. IN TROUBLE

CHAPTER NINE
THE HAUNTED BOAT

Everyone turned their heads away from the boat, looking terrified. I had no idea what was going on but was certainly in no position to go against the majority so I too turned away. Trembling, Ning told me, "No matter what happens, don't turn around. Even if something touches you, pretend it's not happening."

"Don't frighten me like that—why would anything touch me?"

She glanced at me and whispered, "Listen to me, you fool. In a minute you'll find out for yourself."

She sounded as though she was talking about black magic, and the crew's pale and frightened faces gave credence to her words. I whispered, "But you still haven't told me what this is?"

"Shut up for God's sake. These are spirits of those who died before their time and have come to steal our lives for themselves."

The more she talked, the more horrified I became. My neck muscles began to involuntarily turn around for a quick peek; I pinched my thigh in order to tighten my neck, making it as stiff and immobile as though it were encased in a plaster cast.

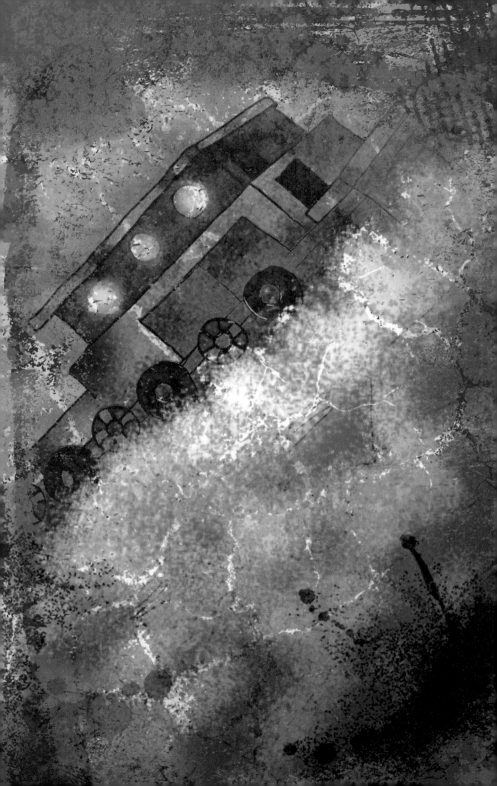

Our boat was rocking fiercely, creaking as though it was going to fall apart any minute. My hands clung to a railing above the deck with my butt braced firmly to keep from losing my footing, but my torso continued to follow the motion of the boat, swinging back and forth like a horse's tail. My body was drenched with seawater and my hands were so cold it was hard for them to keep their grip—I was sure I would soon be hurled into the angry waves that surrounded us.

Thumping, squeaking noises came from the haunted boat, sounding like footsteps echoing on its deck. "What's that noise? Are those footsteps? Could this perhaps be a normal boat that's in trouble?"

In reply, Ning gestured with her chin, directing my gaze to the window of our boat's cabin. Reflected in the glass was a fishing boat the same size as ours that was buffeted by waves. As it drew closer, I could see that it was covered by a thick coating of rust, indicating that this vessel had been at sea for decades. How could it still be afloat after all that time? And how could it still have oil to illuminate the lamp that glowed from it through the darkness?

In novels, haunted boats were dilapidated but still seaworthy—but this one looked like scrap metal dredged up from the depths of the sea. Never had I ever read about a boat that looked this bad.

The boat came closer and closer, much too close for safety's sake and I whispered to Ning, "That boat plans to ram us. Tell the captain to change his course at once."

"Our captain will turn when he thinks the time is right. Our boat weighs about two tons, so don't worry about it being hit. Just hold on and don't fall."

I couldn't tell from her tone of voice whether she was genuinely concerned about me or if she was being sarcastic. I said, "What will we do if he jumps off to save himself?"

"Don't be such a jerk—this boat is the captain's livelihood—he'd never abandon it," Miss Ning said angrily. "If you keep talking, I'll push you overboard!"

I shut up and concentrated on the reflection of the haunted boat in the glass. It approached us so slowly that I realized there would be little impact if it struck. As it came closer, I saw that there was nothing on board and sighed in relief. I closed my eyes and gritted my teeth in preparation for the collision.

Then everything grew quiet. Nothing hit us; nothing happened. After a few seconds of complete silence, I heard the thumps and creaks behind me once again and peeked quickly at the reflection in the window. The haunted boat was floating beside us and there was nothing behind me at all.

I glanced at Ning and saw that she too was staring at the reflection, eyes fixed upon something that I couldn't see. I moved closer to her so I could share her viewpoint and saw two emaciated, withered hands hanging over her shoulders.

CHAPTER TEN
THE DEADLY HANDS

These hands looked human, as thin as two pieces of dried kindling, hanging limp and motionless as though they were part of Ning's wet suit. Just looking at them was horrible; I couldn't imagine what Ning was feeling as she stood, trembling violently in their grasp. I was amazed that she hadn't fainted from terror.

The captain was kneeling on the deck with his back toward us, kowtowing and chanting something in his own language. I thought he was probably performing a ritual to ask for his ancestors' blessing and protection. He took two strange-looking semicircular pieces of wood from his pocket and tossed them onto the deck as if he was asking the gods to help us. He looked at the results of his throw, kowtowed a few more times, picked up the pieces of wood, and tossed them again. I saw his body begin to shiver and deduced that the results hadn't made him feel reassured.

Then Ning screamed as she was pulled backward; quickly the hands dragged her on board the haunted boat, which began to float away from us. I ran to the helm, ready to change our course and pursue the fleeing vessel, but the captain grabbed me from behind, shouting, "There's nothing we can do! Now that she's on the haunted boat, it's impossible to rescue her. Don't be a fool—you'll only sacrifice yourself for nothing."

I struggled in a rage but couldn't break free from the captain's grip. The crew seemed caught in a spell, their heads still averted from everything that was happening, but Baldy erupted into view. He pulled up our anchor and tossed its hook with all of his might toward the haunted boat. It caught the railing of the deck and the rope that attached it to our vessel pulled taut, drawing us closer to Ning.

Cursing wildly, the captain panicked, took out a knife, and was ready to cut us free from the anchor's tether, but Baldy knocked him to the deck with one well-placed punch. The crew, released from their trance, came to help their leader, but Baldy pulled out a pistol, pointed it at the captain, and yelled, "Don't move, or I'll kill him!"

The crew froze and Baldy yelled to me, "Young Wu, I have them under control—now quick, go and rescue Ning!"

I shook my head. He was out of his mind. I was no athlete, and for me to jump into the sea would be the end of me. If I were crazy enough to clamber along the rope that attached us to the boat and managed to safely get to the other side, I'd be lucky to have one breath left in my body. I'd certainly be in no shape for a rescue.

Then I saw Ning, shrieking on the deck of the haunted boat. She was struggling desperately to climb onto the rope but she was being pulled back by something I couldn't see. Grabbing tightly to the side of the boat with both hands, she shrieked, "Mr. Wu! Please help me!"

Her plea slapped me in the face and I cursed at myself, "Fuck it, am I a man or not?"

Maybe it was her cry that inspired my change of heart or perhaps I followed Baldy into insanity, but I took a deep breath, grabbed a pair of goggles, kicked off my shoes, and grabbed the rope that shackled the two boats together. I pulled myself onto the thick hawser and began to edge my way into a world of stormy water and towering waves. Slowly and painfully I crawled, hanging upside down, clinging desperately to the safety of the rope with both of my arms and legs.

Waves crashed into my body, choking me and submerging me in saltwater. At first I struggled against suffocation, and then I understood how to prevail against this dreadful force. When the waves buffeted my body, I stopped moving. When they moved on, I climbed forward once more, working with the sea's rhythm instead of fighting against it.

It seemed as though I'd been in the water for days before I finally neared my goal. Suddenly a mountainous wave struck me, engulfing my entire body, and I plunged deep under the water's surface, almost passing out from the force of the breaker.

Holding my breath, I forced myself to open my eyes. Before me was the bottom of the ghostly vessel and hanging from it was a very long, rust-covered chain. A weird object hung from it which I could see dimly through the depths of the water.

As I tried to look closer, the rope that I clung to rose upward and I was lifted to the crest of the wave. Looking down, I saw Ning, motionless and apparently unconscious, being pulled by those two withered, ghostly hands into the cabin of the haunted boat. When I saw this, I moved as fast as I could and stumbled aboard the boat, where I fell on the deck, almost unconscious myself.

10. THE DEADLY HANDS

CHAPTER ELEVEN
WEN-JIN'S GIFT

The deck, corroded by years of rust, groaned beneath my weight but I had no time to worry about any structural flaws. Ning was already halfway inside the dark cabin. Grabbing her legs, I pulled her toward me with every ounce of energy I had left. She was limp deadweight and hard to get a grip on because of her slippery wet suit. Inch by inch, she was still being pulled down a narrow stairwell into the cabin.

I threw myself on top of her body, clinging to her waist as I tugged at her. Now that my weight was combined with hers, I was sure those frail sticklike hands wouldn't be able to maintain their grasp.

But the minute I threw my weight upon Ning, the deck collapsed beneath us, plunging the two of us into the cabin below. We landed with a hard jolt and I sat up shaking. Ning, revived by the fall, was shouting at me, "Get up— you're crushing me to death!"

I found that I was perched on her butt and hastily removed myself, while thinking this wasn't so bad. Usually in horror movies the woman was always on top but I didn't mind this deviation from the conventional scene one bit. As Ning struggled to sit up, I could no longer see the hands that had clung to her shoulders and asked, "Where did those damn hands go?"

She touched her shoulders with a look of puzzled relief. "I don't know," she replied. "After we fell I was so dazed and dizzy I wasn't aware of anything except you squashing me flat."

I shook my head. "Those hands that were dragging you into the cabin weren't figments of our imaginations—they were real and it's impossible that they would dissolve into nothing. The fall must have jolted them off your shoulders—look and see if you're lying on top of them."

Ning looked sick and quickly got up to take a look at what might be under her. There was nothing. "Maybe they slipped off when we fell; I noticed they were hanging onto the steps going down to the cabin before the deck gave way."

The two of us looked around the cabin; light streamed through the hole we had made by crashing through the deck. The inner walls were encased in layers of white rust, which covered everything inside. We cut through layers of rust that shrouded unidentifiable objects and found navigation instruments, so rotten that they would probably shatter if we touched them.

Judging by the appearance and the spaciousness of the cabin, I estimated this iron-hulled fishing boat had been built thirty or forty years ago. It was divided by a wall into what looked like the crew's lounge, the captain's quarters, and the cargo compartment, which was probably where we were standing. We saw nothing that showed how the boat had come to the sad condition it was in now.

Ning shook her head and said, "I know quite a bit about boats but this one baffles all common sense. It's so rusted that I would say it must have been under the sea for over a decade."

I asked, "Could the storm have brought it back up to the water's surface?"

"I doubt it," she replied. "Anything on the bottom of the sea for ten years or more would be completely buried in sand by now. It would be difficult to resurrect even with heavy equipment to lift it. Besides, the hull of this boat is fragile at this point and will fall into bits if not carefully handled."

There was no immediate answer to why a sunken vessel would be afloat once more, but at least the hands were gone so I could calm down a bit. I stood up and beckoned for Ning to join me in looking around the cabin. The dividing wall was old and rotten and I moved my foot back to give it a good kick. Ning grabbed my arm and warned, "This is a supporting wall connected to the deck. If you kick it, I'm afraid the entire deck will fall down."

In the middle of the wall was a closed door; I yanked at it a couple of times and it fell into pieces, revealing a room that contained a large iron bed frame with a metal cabinet nearby. It was locked but so badly corroded that I was able to open it without any trouble and found an old waterproof bag.

I opened it and out fell a tattered and disintegrating notebook. On its cover was written "Archaeological Record of the Xisha Reefs."

I flipped to the title page and saw, inscribed in graceful, elegant handwriting: "July 1984—For Chen Wen-Jin, from Wu Sansheng."

CHAPTER TWELVE
MY UNCLE, THE LIAR

What the hell, I thought, could this be Uncle Three's book? Why is it on this boat?

Let's assume that before this boat sank, there had been two people on it who just happened to be named Wu Sansheng and Chen Wen-Jin. And let's suppose that these two people had also come to the reefs of Xisha on an archaeological expedition twenty years ago—and that they just happened to have the same names as Uncle Three and his long-lost love. The chances of these coincidences occurring were so slim that it would be the same as if I won a five-million-yuan lottery three times in a row.

No matter how hard I thought, there was no other valid explanation for this notebook—it had to have been left behind by my uncle and his group. The inscription told me that Uncle Three had given the book to Wen-Jin as a present and that she had used it to record a daily log of their expedition.

Obviously this haunted boat had been part of Uncle Three's ill-fated adventure; perhaps it had been the larger fishing boat that carried their dead comrade to shore and didn't return in time to save them from the tsunami.

So many questions came with this notebook that my head began to split. There were only a few people who could provide answers to what was plaguing me—all I had was a shadow of the truth with nothing solid to link my theories together. If only that old bastard of an uncle had told me the whole story to begin with, I would probably have the key to the entire mystery now.

Perhaps this notebook had the clues I needed; I opened it and began to read.

Wen-Jin was a diligent record keeper—she wrote in the same style every day, neatly and clearly. The book began with the day they set out on their expedition—July 15. She recorded everybody's names and that son of a bitch Wu Sansheng, aka Uncle Three, really was the leader.

What was Poker-face called? I vaguely remembered Uncle Three telling me his last name was Zhang—so I checked from top to bottom, and sure enough there was someone named Zhang Qilin. I remembered the tattoo of the qilin that I saw on Poker-face's bloody back in the cave of the zombies and thought holy shit, could that really be him?

I flipped the pages again. The first part of Wen-Jin's log described how the group had located and identified the undersea tomb. This was a much more detailed account than the one I'd received from my uncle. Wen-Jin carefully recorded everything, right down to the kind of ropes they used. She was the polar opposite of that uneducated, haphazard fool, Uncle Three, and I couldn't figure out how the two of them had ever become attracted to each other.

Eager to know what had befallen the group, I turned to the last page of the notebook—and then I wished I hadn't.

All I needed to read were a few lines of Wen-Jin's account to be completely horrified—my uncle was a son of a bitch magnified to the hundredth power.

"July 21," she wrote in her careful script, "First time into the undersea tomb. Crew: Wu Sansheng. Progress: Cleared the left ear chamber and corridor. Preparing to clean up back chamber. Work: Changed ventilation of tomb with the use of an air pump. Preparing for a lengthier cleanup. Relics obtained: Gold wooden coffin carved with dual phoenix and eagle (infant coffin). Note: Emergency event, detailed records to be completed at a later time."

Then there was only one more entry: "July 23, Second time into the undersea tomb. Crew: All members. Progress: None. Work: To avoid monsoon storm. Relics obtained: None. Note: None."

So Uncle Three had entered the tomb once before they all went in together. With his flair for looting and plundering, he must have taken the opportunity to appropriate his share and more. Wen-Jin only wrote down here that he had carried out the cleaning of the ear chamber and the corridor. But who would ever find out whether he had entered the back chamber or not? He had probably already taken the treasures in the coffin.

I rapidly skimmed the journal; there were many useful details in the records, but they weren't significant enough that I needed to read them carefully right now. I put the notebook back into the waterproof bag and looked over at Ning, who was paying no attention to me or my discovery. Instead she was vigorously trying to strip off the layer of sea rust on the wall that formed a partition in the captain's chamber.

She moved quickly, as if she were not just trying to peel away the layer but to smash it to bits. She had cleaned off half the wall, and I could see that under the sea rust was steel. She continued stripping to the point where the hull and the partition were joined, and we could see that all four sides of this wall were welded to the steel hull. The door on the partition was also made of steel, with a spinning security lock attached to it that looked like the steering wheel of a car.

As she scraped, Ning muttered, "Don't be afraid. Don't be afraid. I'll let you out soon."

Was this woman out of it or what? I watched her somewhat warily as she neatly scraped away all the sea rust and uncovered a layer of rubber placed between the door and the frame to make an airtight seal. Ning began diligent efforts to turn the wheel that locked the door but her strength wasn't up to the job.

Not only was the wheel heavy and difficult to turn, but the lock was so corroded that only a muscle-bound sailor would have been able to open it.

"Let's leave this alone." I tried to stop Ning. "We have no idea what's behind that door and we have no weapons to use in case some sort of monster is lurking there. I don't want to die, do you?"

Ning continued to wrestle with the wheel without replying, and I began to regret I had ever come to her rescue. I folded my arms and fumed at her obstinacy, watching her waste her strength and our time. When she turned to look at me, I was sure she was ready to give up and leave this place but instead she tilted backward, screaming.

The two ghastly hands emerged from beneath her hair and gripped the wheel of the lock. From behind the door I could hear the sound of huge clumps of rusted iron falling to the floor of the deck.

So that's where those damn hands were hiding. I shuddered silently and wondered who was muttering "I'll let you out" a minute ago: this woman or a ghost?

The lock opened and the hideous hands tugged at the door. Then with a loud crash, an onslaught of water swept toward the door and flung it wide open, hitting Ning on the back. She flew backward toward me and we both fell flat on the deck. Before I could get up, a wave crashed over us, striking my head and pushing us farther back. Looking up, I saw a gigantic face, covered with fish scales, staring at us from the open door.

CHAPTER THIRTEEN
THE SEA MONKEY

The face was nearly four or five times larger than my entire head. Its body was hidden behind the steel door, so I couldn't tell how big it was. The light shining through the damaged deck was dim and I was unable to decide whether this was the face of an animal or a ghost.

I was so frightened that I tingled from my scalp to my ankles and my legs were as soft as noodles. It took all the strength I had to take a few steps backward, determined to get away somehow—and then I saw Ning lying at my feet, unconscious again. Although she wasn't my favorite person in the world at the moment, abandoning her was certainly not the right thing to do.

I raised her head and saw that once again the hands had disappeared, but I had no time to worry about where they were. I grabbed Ning under her arms and slowly dragged her toward the safety of the stairs. If I could pull her up onto what was left of the deck, we could plunge into the sea and I could shriek for rescue—a better situation than the one we were in now.

Calm down, calm down, I told myself, it's not as though you haven't faced this sort of situation before—you're an experienced grave robber after all. With my eyes fixed upon the scale-covered face, I stepped backward very slowly.

Whatever the monster was, it remained motionless, eyes fixed upon me, which made it more terrifying than if it sprang into attack. Get a grip, I thought, as long as it's still, the more of a chance you have to escape. I tore my gaze from its stare and dragged Ning to the bottom of the stairs. But that was no refuge—the steps had rotted away, leaving only a banister to cling to. How could I manage to climb up to the deck, especially when burdened with the baggage I had taken on?

There were still a few pieces of metal that had once supported the steps. Pulling Ning by her arms, I put my foot on one, but it dissolved beneath my feet like soggy mud.

The monster watched us, patiently waiting for me to give up, but I was at a point where I could see the edges of the hole in the deck. I propped Ning against the wall and, gritting my teeth, I leaped toward the opening.

My arms were long but my strength had dwindled to nothing during the exertions of the past hour or so. I missed the top of the opening twice and fell flat on my face each time I tried. Almost in tears from pain, anger, and humiliation, I sat in a state of complete despair, then turned to check on the monster.

It would have been better if I hadn't. Its face was right behind me, so close that our heads almost touched.

Imagine if you turned to find a man unexpectedly standing behind you in silence. That was me—but what I saw was inhuman and horrible. I began to scream and move away until my back was against the wall.

13. THE SEA MONKEY

I had nowhere else to go.

The monster reminded me of a story that a classmate had told me when I was a boy. He said that once a fisherman found a weird creature in his net that looked like a man but was covered with scales. He took it to his village where an old man screamed, "Let this go at once! This is a sea monkey—if you keep it, its band will come to save him and we'll all be in danger."

When the fisherman heard this, he decided the sea monkey was probably valuable and felt sure he could sell it in the city for a high price. So he told everyone he had let the creature go, while really he hid it in his house. The next day, the fisherman's entire family disappeared and after searching for two days, villagers found the body of the fisherman's wife under a seaside cliff. Her stomach was ripped open and all her internal organs had been devoured.

When the old man saw what had happened, he knew the other sea monkeys had come for revenge. He called upon a Feng Shui master, set up a sacrificial platform, beheaded a lot of pigs and goats, and performed ceremonies for several days.

My classmate drew a sketch of the sea monkey to show me the way it looked. He was good at drawing and his picture made a huge impression on me, giving me several sleepless nights. What my friend had drawn was now standing in front of me, exactly as he had drawn it but much, much larger and much more hideous.

The sea monkey stood still, staring at Ning and drooling. It was a good thing she was still unconscious or she'd be peeing her pants in terror. I was sure she would because I was almost doing the same thing myself.

I forced myself to calm down, pressing my body firmly against the wall, which was as rotten and spongy as everything else on this damn boat. A plan began to emerge as I pushed. If I kept this up, I could probably make a hole in the wall which would be a sanctuary if the sea monkey decided to attack me.

As I pushed and plotted, I suddenly heard creaking noises coming from the deck as if someone had just climbed on board and then Baldy, of all people, leaped through the hole in the deck. Looking at the open door, he raised a pistol, then turned, saw the sea monkey and screamed, "Shit!"

The sea monkey bellowed and leaped toward Baldy, who quickly moved away, aimed, and fired. His bullet hit the monster in the shoulder and it reeled back against the wall. Quickly Baldy shot a round of bullets that narrowly missed me—and the sea monkey. The monster raced off through the open door, slammed it shut, and clicked the lock back into place.

Baldy kept shooting. On the wall appeared a line of bullet holes, and water began to gush into the cabin. Although the water rose rapidly around us, Baldy was still out for blood. He fired a couple of shots that broke the door's hinges and then he kicked it open.

We both rushed through and discovered a hole in the deck that the sea monkey was trying to push its body through. It was extremely strong; as Baldy aimed at it again, it slammed its head against the deck to make the hole big enough to accommodate its size and disappeared into the sea below.

The boat groaned as though it were breaking apart. We stood in water up to our knees. Baldy ran back to our unconscious companion. "Ning, Ning," he called as he shook her gently, but there was no response. He flung her over his shoulders, climbed up on my back, and made it to the deck above. Their combined weights nearly destroyed me and I choked back rising bile as Baldy reached down and pulled me up to safety.

CHAPTER FOURTEEN
AN OLD FRIEND

As soon as I was on the deck, I heard an eerie, ominous sound echoing through the boat and saw that the two ends of the boat were on different levels. The keel was gone, which meant the hull was bound to crack and we would be underwater in a very few minutes.

"Look, there's our boat. Let's get off this damn thing now," Baldy yelled. And then I could see it too, with the captain shouting, "Are you guys okay?"

Because the haunted boat had taken on so much water, it was moving slowly and our boat was soon beside it. Two of the crew jumped over to carry Ning to safety, their faces clearly showing their reluctance to be on board the boat they feared so much. We followed them quickly, and the captain shouted, "Hoist the anchor so we can leave this place right now."

Ning lay sprawled on the deck, and the captain told me to hold her head in my arms as he ruffled his hands through her short, thick hair.

Hiding there were two arms, old and wrinkled, twisted in her hair. They were short and at their rotting ends was a small tumor that somehow was attached to Ning's scalp. The side that was turned toward us bore a contorted little face.

The captain kowtowed several times, took something from his pocket, and sprinkled it on the tiny face, which shrieked and grimaced in pain. Then the captain took out a knife, sliced the face from the tumor, and pulled the mass of flesh off Ning's scalp. It fell on the deck, twisting and curling, then melted into a gluey, starchlike liquid and drained through the cracks in the planks.

"What the hell?" I muttered and the captain replied very quietly, "This is a face demon. I got rid of it with some hair from an ox, which is the only way to destroy it."

He rinsed his knife clean in some saltwater and muttered something I couldn't hear. It was plain that he wished he had never signed up for this voyage.

The sea had calmed and the clouds that had darkened the sky were breaking up, with shafts of sunlight coming through. The captain went to the upper deck and I knew he was watching the sea, looking for the sea monkey that might follow us to take its revenge.

The crew had gone back to work and Ning was safe in a corner of the boat. As I calmed down, exhaustion struck and I slept until sunset.

I awoke to find our boat sailing along the coast of an island with a gleaming beach of white sand. We were approaching a small pier where it was apparent we were going to dock.

Surprised that we were going ashore so soon, I asked, "What's up?"

"We're going to pick up a few people here on Yongxing Island," a familiar voice said and I turned to see Ning, conscious at last and with color back in her face, looking quite appealing.

I can't resist a pretty woman and even though she still had a fragile tinge to her appearance, my little companion was sexier than I'd realized before, when she was causing me so much trouble. Smiling as beguilingly as I could, I asked, "Who's joining us?"

She pointed toward the pier and said, "Them—a few divers and a consultant, like you. I'm pretty sure you know him."

I stared hard at the approaching figures. One of them—a rotund fellow—looked familiar but I couldn't place him. A crew member standing on the bow of the boat shouted, "Ahoy! Get a move on—we're waiting."

The round figure turned toward us and cursed, "Ahoy my ass! I've been sitting here for half an hour gulping down this northwest wind that almost blew my face off. Don't you goddamn people have any fucking sense of time?"

CHAPTER FIFTHEEN
FATS

What the hell, I thought, it's Fats. He was bulkier than he had been when I last saw him a couple of weeks before but as energetic as ever. Our boat neared the pier but didn't stop—Fats ran to the edge of the dock and with one leap landed on our deck.

When he caught sight of me, he burst into a huge grin. "Hey, here you are, with the famous Miss Ning." Ning smiled back at him. I didn't know whether to be relieved or pissed off that Fats had joined us—my feelings about this guy had always been mixed. When I thought of the times he had nearly killed me on our last adventure, I began to have a really bad headache.

Throwing his bag on the deck, Fats sat across from me. He rubbed his shoulders and grinned again. "I was in one hell of a rush to get here—you guys didn't give me much time to get ready. Have you found the location yet?"

Miss Ning shook her head. "No, but we're pretty sure of where it is."

"Look," Fats told her, "I've already explained this once. I'm not the kind of guy who fucks around with Feng Shui principles—searching for the dragon, attacking its vital point, detecting the locale, or fixing the position. I go to work only after you locate the spot. No skin off my ass if you can't find it. I still get paid my money either way. This is the way we do things in the real world—you southern yokels need to get a clue before you start messing around outside your comfort zone."

Obviously annoyed, Ning exhaled sharply and snapped, "I already know what you will and will not do. We've arranged for Mr. Wu to be responsible for finding the specific location."

What the fuck? I was responsible? What was I responsible for? They hadn't even handed me a shovel yet, let alone any sort of game plan. "What are you talking about? Don't you people even know where this underground tomb is?"

"We can only estimate the approximate location," Ning told me. "If we can find the robbers' cave, then great. If we can't, we'll have to rely on you to pinpoint the exact location and determine the shape of the undersea tomb. We have some data from a heap of old papers, but that's no substitute for the knowledge of an experienced grave robber. Your uncle was very secretive and left us nothing to go on."

Well shit, I thought, it seems as though I was going to be up all night, trying to remember everything my grandfather had ever told me so I wouldn't look like a complete idiot the next day.

I would have no problem with the actual digging—if I made any mistakes at the bottom of the sea, I could always blame the water. After all, grave robbing on dry land was quite different from practicing the art on the ocean's bed, and I was not a master of the underwater world. But I had no idea of how to map out a grave, although I had carefully observed Uncle Three at work, which had to count as some sort of experience. I began to relax. This would all work out and if it didn't, I'd use the tomb's poor construction as an alibi.

Fats glanced my way and said, "Good—let's be sure to have a delicious dinner tonight so we have enough energy for the work that waits for us tomorrow. Hey, Captain—is there any fresh fish on this boat of yours?"

Miss Ning seemed to have no interest in his suggestion but I was ravenous. When I heard Fats mention seafood, my mouth began to water and I joined him to find out what we might have for dinner.

People often said that the sea we sailed through was half water, half fish, and we were on a fishing boat which was well supplied with Spanish mackerel, flutefish, and grouper. As Fats bellowed and badgered, the captain rather grouchily took a huge mackerel from the freezer, handed it to one of the crew, and said, "Put this in the pot right now."

Fats looked offended and muttered, "God damn it, stop acting as though I'm robbing you of your hard-earned money." But once the fish was cooked, it smelled so delicious that he and the captain both got over their bad moods and I could think of nothing but filling my stomach.

The smell of the fish brought Baldy up on deck, drawing close to the pot and sniffing at it hungrily. "The sea is marvelous just because of this—you can pull up a fish, cook it in a simple fashion, and eat something you would never taste anywhere else, no matter where you lived or how wealthy you might be."

Fats grabbed at his sleeve yelling, "For God's sake, go blather somewhere else. Don't slobber into the pot or you'll ruin our dinner."

Baldy looked at Fats and realized he'd never seen him before. He held out his hand, saying, "Ah, a new face, how may I address you?"

Always outspoken, Fats turned to Ning and asked, "Who's this bald moron?"

Baldy's face reddened and he snapped, "Please call me Mr. Zhang or Professor Zhang, okay?"

Fats ignored him. Ning hurried to calm the tension, saying, "I'm so sorry, this is my fault. I forgot to introduce you. This is Professor Zhang, another consultant on this expedition."

Fats was immediately impressed by the academic title and eagerly shook Baldy's hand. "Ah—I am truly sorry. I didn't know that you were an intellectual. My last name is Wang. I'm just a country boy, a simple straight-speaking guy. Please don't be offended."

Baldy smiled cautiously. "Both intellectuals and yokels are humans. Intellectuals are simply yokels transformed. It's just a matter of different divisions of labor."

Fats had no idea of what Baldy was talking about and looked confused as he was asked, "So what line of work are you in, Mr. Wang?"

"Oh that—to put it simply, I work underground."

Baldy was awestruck at his reply and said, "You're an undercover policeman. My apologies."

I snorted to keep from bursting into laughter. Fats looked at me menacingly and said, "Let's not talk now.

Have a bite or two first," and he motioned for us all to start our meal.

After a few mouthfuls of the fish, Fats began to yell for drinks. "This is a fishing boat," Ning said. "There's no alcohol on board." But Fats paid no attention. Rushing into the cabin, he began to toss things around and came out with a bottle of wine from the altar of the captain's shrine.

"Put that down at once, you fool," the captain yelled as he rushed toward Fats. "That's a gift for the Dragon Prince, the god of the sea."

Fats was furious. "What bullshit are you giving me? The Dragon Prince would certainly destroy your boat if you gave him this lousy wine."

From his bag he took out a bottle of liquor and jammed it into the captain's hands. "Take this, and present it to His Highness of the Seas. This is what's called a cultural exchange between the north and south. You see that? Red Star Double Pot—it's good stuff. Don't refuse it, God damn it."

The captain stood still and speechless as Fats opened the bottle that had been on the altar and poured a glass of wine for each of us. It was a small-town specialty, coconut wine, and it was undeniably good. We ate and drank like pigs until the moon was well above our heads.

Fats took a last gulp of wine, belched, and announced, "All right everybody. Now that our bellies are full, let's get serious."

CHAPTER SIXTEEN
CONFERENCE

Fats gave off an energetic enthusiasm that made me excited too. I knew from being with him in the cavern of the blood zombies that although he was a bit flaky, he had guts and creativity. And he was a much more experienced grave robber than I was, so I was eager to hear what he had to say.

Rubbing his bulging stomach, he began, "I've never been down to an undersea tomb before so I want a lot of preparation before we begin this adventure—what sort of equipment do you have for us?"

"Considering your lack of experience, Mr. Wang," Ning said sharply, "how confident can we be in your abilities? Why don't we hear your plan of action so we know what to expect from you."

Fats shook his head and looked thoughtful. "It's hard to say. Based on my experience, the first problem to solve is the difficulty of finding the location of this tomb; then we face the excavation challenge. Most important are what dangers we may encounter once we're inside—we have no idea if there are zombies waiting for us. If there are, we're in deep shit. If not, then it's a straightforward job—get in and get out with whatever treasure we may find there."

When he mentioned zombies, I recalled what Uncle Three had told me about the monster he had encountered in the tunnel years ago. The more I thought about it, the more I suspected it was the sea monkey I saw today.

"I don't know if there are any zombies but there may be something that's even more threatening." And then I told them about the creature I saw earlier, about which Baldy had already given an exaggerated account, elaborating upon all the heroic exploits he been forced to perform in order to save Ning and me. After hearing my more accurate and realistic version, Fats frowned and asked, "Holy shit. So this fucker really exists?"

I nodded. "There are legends about it all over China— too many different regions have seen this for me to think it doesn't exist."

Ning nodded as she backed me up. "I heard about it when I was a child, but I thought it was a story made up by the grown-ups to keep us kids from playing beside the river."

She was interrupted by the captain. "No, no. You guys don't know the first thing about this. All the fishermen around here have seen this creature. Let me tell you, these are not sea monkeys—they're Yaksha ghosts—relatives of the Dragon Prince. Now that you've injured one, he most certainly will come back for revenge. I think we should hurry to shore, buy a pig, return, and hire a Taoist priest to perform a ceremony. Perhaps His Eminence will be merciful enough to spare our lives."

Fats laughed derisively and replied, "Now that we know there is such a creature down on the seabed, we certainly need to have weapons with us. What if that undersea tomb is its nest? Then won't we be running to our deaths? Miss Ning, did you bring spearguns?"

"We've considered the possibility of this sort of danger, and prepared a number of spearguns. But these guns are unwieldy, and each can be used only once before it needs to be reloaded. I am afraid they won't be too useful in a real emergency."

I knew that this was a gun that used compressed air to propel its missiles. Its range was only several feet but luckily it could also be used as an old-fashioned spear. However, it was too long to be useful in the narrow tunnels of a tomb.

Fats ignored her, shouting, "You can never have too many guns. Bring as many as you have. I'll lead the crew tomorrow when we dive down. Young comrade Wu will follow me. You and that bald guy stay in the back. If I see something wrong, I'll wave my hand, and you guys stop immediately. If I make a fist, then drop everything and escape right away."

We thought it was a relatively sound arrangement and went on to discuss other things. I called to mind some of the experiences Uncle Three had been through, and from his accounts I put together a list of things we might need: searchlights, daggers, matches, sealed waterproof bags, nylon ropes, food, first aid supplies, gas masks, toolboxes—even a black donkey hoof to strip vampires of their powers.

Our planning kept us awake almost until daybreak, when Fats pointed out if we didn't stop talking and get some rest, we'd never get into the water. The coconut wine had been strong. My head was heavy and I slept until noon.

16. CONFERENCE

The others were already awake and gathering their gear. As I washed my face with seawater, several divers floated up to the surface, took off their respirators, and said, "We got it. It's definitely the place. We even found the opening of the cave."

"Did you go in to take a look?" Ning asked.

The diver shook his head and said, "Yes, but the tunnel looked very long. I went down for a bit, couldn't see the end, and didn't dare continue, so we came back up."

Ning nodded and said to us, "Okay. Let's get ready," and after double-checking our equipment to make sure we had everything we needed, we disappeared into the depths of the sea.

CHAPTER SEVENTEEN
FACES OF STONE

It took only a few minutes to reach the cave. Someone had used dynamite recently to blow a large pit in the seabed, and at the bottom of it was the opening to the cave. It certainly looked like Uncle Three's work to me.

A few stone anchors lay scattered around but it was impossible to tell if they were the same ones my uncle had told me about. The outlines of the tomb that Uncle Three had surveyed were still clearly visible. We investigated the cave opening to be sure it hadn't been destabilized by the explosion, but it looked fine—apparently Uncle Three's skills were still impeccable.

Fats waved to me as a signal to enter the cave's tunnel. Ning glanced at her watch and nodded her agreement. We all followed Fats as he disappeared into the opening and in seconds we were below the floor of the sea.

The structure of the tunnel was very irregular, sometimes wide, sometimes painfully narrow. It looked as though it had been dug by a dog to hide his bone, rather than the careful and orderly work of grave robbers.

We swam beyond the range of the light that came through the cave's opening. Suddenly, the direction of the tunnel changed, becoming steeply vertical, and we stopped to take a quick break. Fats gestured for us to be careful and then he swam down alone. He beckoned that it was safe to follow and one by one, we plunged back down into the tunnel.

There were the walls of the tomb, with a large hole leading within. I looked at it, puzzled. Unlike the careful process used by grave robbers of dismantling a wall brick by brick, the shape of this hole was irregular, with many of the bricks badly cracked. Pointing at the damaged bricks, Fats took on the motions of a monkey and I understood. This hole might not be the beginning of a robbers' tunnel; it could be the work of a sea monkey. Nodding, I pointed to the speargun on his back. He took it from its sheath, cocked it, and swam toward the hole.

This was the second time I had entered an ancient tomb. Although I was excited, I recalled my last experience and felt a bit uneasy. We were on the bottom of the sea, where the pressure of the water made it difficult to move. If there was any danger, I was afraid we wouldn't be able to escape as quickly as we would on land.

The grave tunnel was much more spacious than I had imagined. I turned on my waterproof flashlight and followed Fats's butt. We carried lots of light, so the grave tunnel was well illuminated. I looked at the walls of the tomb and sure enough, they were carved with the human faces Uncle Three had described. They were all finely and exquisitely fashioned with a strange animal embossed on each face, beasts that were traditional guardians of graves. None of them had eyes carved in their heads, which gave them an eerie appearance.

17. FACES OF STONE

Suddenly I saw carved on one of the human faces something that looked like three of the Bronze Fish with Snake Brows. My heart grew tight in my chest, and I hurriedly pulled at Fats to stop while I swam over to examine the face.

Not knowing what I had found, Fats impatiently beckoned for me to keep going but I ignored him. The three fish were connected from end to end in a ring. Two were like the ones in my bag while the third had three eyes. The face that the fish were carved upon was female with soft, delicate features. I wanted to examine it more closely, but Ning was urging me to get a move on so I had no alternative but to continue swimming.

Fortunately, that same face reappeared as I swam along and I could still peek at it. Somehow it gave the tunnel an unpleasant feeling and I found out why when it appeared on a wall the fifth time.

The first face I saw had her eyes closed. The one on the second wall seemed to have opened them a little. On the third and fourth faces, the eyes opened wider and wider. Now, on the fifth one, the eyes were nearly gaping at me.

I pulled Fats to a stop, took out my underwater drawing board, and wrote, "The eyes of these faces carved on the walls are gradually opening. It's a bad sign—pay attention!"

Fats shook his head and wrote, "What's the problem? These are only stone carvings, not living beings—you think too much. You always do."

I shook my head and made him take out his spear. A moment later, I saw the same carving again. By now Fats was a little shaken by what I had told him. He stopped and pointed his searchlight at the carving. The eyes on that face were completely open, staring ahead. Fats moved the light back and forth, gathered up his courage, and touched the carving. He made a gesture to me as if to say there was nothing wrong.

I swam over. Sure enough, it was just a hunk of rock— nothing special about it. I poked the eyes with my fingers, but they remained immobile. I felt stupid; this had to be a trick put in by the designer of the tomb to frighten any robbers that might enter the tunnel. It certainly had made me lose face.

We continued to swim forward. I remembered Uncle Three had told me that he had hit some sort of trap before being washed into the mysterious room. But all of these tomb walls looked exactly the same. How could I find the one that he had hit?

My mind raced like a caged hamster. Swimming forward blindly wasn't the answer. We didn't know where this tunnel would lead us; it could be a circle and if we got lost in here, we would be doomed.

At this moment, Fats stopped abruptly and I ran into his butt. I thought there must be a problem, pulled my nerves taut, and stuck my head up to have a look. We could go no further. A large panel of slate blocked the way.

The panel was plain with no inscriptions or carvings on it. I groped around it for a while but found no traps. Ning handed me a note: "How can we get past this dead end?"

I replied, "There must be some hidden device nearby that will open the panel. Look around on the walls."

Fats began to knock here and there on the walls and carefully examined human faces that were carved on them. I tried hard to remember the clues mentioned in Wen-Jin's logbook and slid my knife into every crack on the edges of the bricks, but with no success. The panel didn't budge.

Discouraged, I turned around to see if Fats had found anything and discovered that he was standing in a trance. I tapped him on his back and wrote, "What's up?"

With a mystified look on his face, he asked, "Does the sea monkey have long hair?"

I didn't know what he was talking about; I really hadn't paid much attention to the sea monkey's hair. When I thought about it, I seemed to see a bald head covered with scales. "Why?" I asked.

Fats pointed to a crack in the wall. My eyes followed the direction of his finger, and immediately I saw a strand of long black hair floating between the slate panel and the tunnel.

What was this from? I wondered. Could there be a person leaning on the other side of the panel?

Gutsy as always, Fats reached out to pull at the strand but it receded back into the crack. He looked at me and wrote, "There's a ghost behind that panel."

CHAPTER EIGHTEEN
HOMICIDAL HAIR

I had to give Fats credit for courage, if not brains. While I was backing away from the slate panel, grateful for the barrier it provided between the mysterious hair and me, he moved closer to take another look, then swam away rapidly. Turning back to look at me, he shook his fist in the air as though he wanted to hit me. Then I realized he was making the signal to get the hell out of there now.

But nothing was happening, I thought. I turned and saw that the panel was gradually rising with a black mass seeping from beneath it. Oh shit, I told myself, it's that damn hair!

Baldy, Ning, and I stared, unable to move as the blackness approached us, until Fats swam back and pulled us away. He shattered our hypnotic state and we began to match his speed. We swam until we reached the first turn of the tunnel, where Fats brought us to a halt and we all looked back to where we had been. The entire tunnel behind us was filled with thick black hair floating in the water, coming toward us.

Fats muttered an obscenity, held up his speargun, and fired. When he saw his missile become entwined uselessly in hair, he looked as though he was going to have a stroke.

But the dart spear did some damage. The hair seemed to flinch as it was struck and began to thrash about like a snake in agony. As it moved, we could see something emerging from it. It moved backward and released something from its center—a dead man.

He was wearing the same kind of wet suit as the ones we had on and I thought he might have been one of Uncle Three's most recent group of missing people. Black thick hair sprouted from his nose, his mouth, and even his eyes. It was obvious that he had died of suffocation.

Even my teeth felt numb as I looked at his body. That hair was going to choke us too if we didn't get out of here. I turned to urge Fats to lead the way but he was nowhere in sight. Shocked, I looked again and saw him in the distance, signaling for us to follow.

As we swam toward Fats, I felt the oxygen gauge vibrate in my hand. We had been underwater for over half an hour and we'd used a lot of oxygen already. I knew we'd have to rise to the surface soon but first I wanted to find the ear chamber Uncle Three had told me about.

Suddenly Baldy, who had been the last in line, grabbed me and, like a crab, scrambled to get to the front. Catching up with Fats, he pulled him to a stop, glaring at him. He took the lead, swimming clumsily but purposefully. He stopped at a tomb wall that was recessed slightly inward— Fats had pushed against it during his rapid retreat and it had caved in a tiny bit.

I was delighted. It looked as though we were at the end of the long tunnel that Uncle Three had found. This must be the trap he had told me about. I knew once it was triggered, water would gush through the opening, taking us with it. But my uncle and his group had all worn those old-fashioned diving helmets so they had survived. We wore only diving goggles and if we were drawn into the maelstrom of water, I was unsure that our unprotected heads wouldn't be cracked open as we careened into the walls.

I looked back. It appeared that the hair no longer pursued us and I swam over to let the others know, just as Baldy pressed against the weakened portion of the wall. There was no time for any warning as water bubbles rippled into the tunnel. An immense force thrust against my back and pushed me through the hole in the wall.

The water whirled me about and I understood what my uncle meant when he said that his internal organs had all migrated to one side of his body. I felt like laundry in the middle of a spin cycle and soon was so dizzy that I passed out.

When I came to, my head wobbled on my neck like an infant's and every bone in my body felt as though it had shattered. I refocused my vision and saw Fats and the others nearby. They all looked as bad as I did, especially Fats, who was still twirling about like a ballet dancer on drugs.

The walls that surrounded us were made of Han white jade, and since the place was built with such fine material, I was sure we'd reached the inside of the tomb. I paddled my legs to float upward and suddenly my head felt warm. I was out of the water at last and engulfed in darkness.

I switched on my flashlight and carefully examined the chamber that we were in. The tomb was rectangular with angled edges. A map of fifty stars was traced on the ceiling but there was no other roof carving. The room looked simple and chaste.

Since there was no coffin or coffin platform, I was sure this was one of the ear chambers. I searched for an exit but there was only one door on the left that led to an outer corridor.

On the floor of the tomb were many porcelain objects that had accompanied the deceased into death. There were hundreds of them, among them several extremely valuable huge porcelain jars imprinted with dragons flying through the clouds. There were also fresh, wet footprints on the dusty floor, which I hoped I could blame on Uncle Three.

I struck a waterproof match and it burst into flame. Since that proved there was air in the chamber, I motioned for my companions to come out of the water. As Ning made her way over, she immediately saw the footprints and asked, "Who left these behind?"

I frowned; I wasn't sure. These were tiny feet that had left this trail, looking as though they might have been made by a three-year-old child—and who the hell ever heard of a grave-robbing toddler? I called Fats over to have a look.

"Who the hell cares what size it is," he exploded. "The damn thing's abnormal. Take another look."

I looked again and this time saw the print was covered with a film of yellow wax. Scraping some up with my knife, I sniffed and gagged. "This is corpse wax. It's goddamn adipocere."

CHAPTER NINETEEN
THE PORCELAIN JAR

Adipocere, also called grave or corpse wax, is a substance that forms on corpses that have either been immersed in water for a long time or buried in wet soil. It's made from the fat of the soggy corpse and other minerals exuded from tissues during the decomposition process and it covers the body to prevent corruption. The corpses of little children often form adipocere because of their high percentage of body fat and obviously this small body was covered with it—at least on the soles of its feet.

The little footprints led to a corner of the room behind a large porcelain jar, and there they stopped. "Look," I said to Fats. "See how these footprints only go in that direction and then stop? Could the corpse be..."

Before I finished my sentence Fats held his finger to his lips and I fell silent. I followed his gaze and saw the porcelain jar shaking for no apparent reason.

"It's hiding behind that jar," Fats whispered.

"Do you suppose it's a zombie?" I asked. "It's so very small."

"I can't be sure unless we go over to investigate." Fats held up his speargun and waved it at me. Hell, I'm not going over there, I thought, and shook my head emphatically. Fats sighed and called over Baldy, who looked thrilled to be part of the excitement. The two of them walked slowly and quietly toward the jar, and realizing I couldn't let myself look like a wimp in front of Ning, I tagged along after them.

As we drew near, Fats held his flashlight high but the jar obscured whatever was behind it. He nudged it several times with his speargun, and when nothing leaped out in attack, he walked behind the jar. "Damn it," he yelped, "there's nothing here but an empty wooden box."

We all joined him and I immediately recognized what he had found. It was a very tiny coffin the size of a violin case, carved with two phoenixes. It was open and the cover was lying close by; there was no corpse anywhere. "It's not a box," I said, "it's a coffin."

"So this is where that little zombie rests its ugly waxy head," Fats remarked as he trained his flashlight within the coffin. "Hell, based on the way this looks, I'll bet that kid is dripping with treasure. Too bad it's not around here—if I hugged it once or twice, I could probably squeeze a few pearls out of its little belly."

For once he wasn't exaggerating. The coffins of children were usually filled with valuable objects. Jewels and gold often ornamented their corpses and they were frequently given pearls to swallow just before they died to prevent their bodies from rotting.

We tried to find the child's corpse with no success. Shit, Uncle Three probably has it tucked under his arm right now, I told myself.

Fats was reluctant to abandon the search and almost turned the coffin upside down to find something of value.

19. THE PORCELAIN JAR

I grabbed his arm and stopped him. "This coffin isn't only for holding the dead. Don't touch it."

He gave a scornful laugh. "What's got you so worried? Do you think the coffin is going to snap off my arm?"

Ning looked worried and said, "We didn't come here to loot the graves of children. Let's stop messing around here, get to the main tomb, and look for our missing men."

Fats had no choice but to go along with the majority. He began to follow us and then stopped as he stared at me. His mouth moved as though he had something to say but nothing was said. I sighed and snapped, "If you have something to say, God damn it, then spit it out now."

"Well," he muttered, "do you suppose that little zombie could have hidden itself inside the porcelain jar?'

I felt stupid for not thinking of this myself; it was certainly possible.

Fats went on. "A moment ago when I heard the noise near the jar, I thought it sounded like it was coming from inside, but then I thought zombies aren't mice that climb into nearby containers. I was sure I was wrong but maybe I wasn't."

Before I could respond, the big jar suddenly fell over onto the floor. As we stared at it, it wiggled a few times and then rolled right toward us.

CHAPTER TWENTY
THE CORRIDOR OF DEATH

We stared at the jar as it rolled in our direction,
then veered toward the door, hit the frame with a
bang, and came to a stop. We froze in place, unable to
move, as Fats whispered, "Listen, there's something
dreadful in this jar. Let's attack it before it injures us.
We should throw a few spears at the jar and kill what
comes out."

"No," I objected. "Let's just keep going and forget
about this for now."

I knew this jar was a prize find, one of the few giant
blue and white porcelain pieces from the Ming dynasty
that was still unbroken. It would be criminally stupid
to damage it. And I knew our oxygen supplies were
dwindling fast; if there was a zombie in that jar, even
if it was very tiny, we'd still have a fight on our hands
and not enough air to put us on the winning side. And
more than anything, I knew I was close to my physical
limits and was sure the others were too.

"It might just be a lobster or crab hiding in that
jar," Fats wheedled. "Why should we let ourselves be
frightened like this. Let's just go over and take a peek."

Ning shook her head. "We need to get to the main

tomb right now without wasting any more time. Let's avoid the jar by finding another way out of here."

But there was no other exit or even an opening for us to crawl through. When Fats saw this, his face swelled as though he was about to explode. "Damn it, either we move this jar or we're stuck here forever. Maybe you are all cowards but I'll quit this minute rather than be scared stiff by something that might not even be here."

I saw the obstinate expression on Ning's face that I was beginning to know quite well. Fats looked furious and Baldy was blank as usual. The three of them looked at me as if they wanted my opinion.

I didn't really have one. I knew it would be stupid to rush into trouble but Fats had a point. Grave robbers often became consumed by panic just because they had managed to terrify themselves for no reason. "Okay," I decided, "we'll take this one step at a time. If there's no problem, terrific. If we find trouble, I'm carrying four spearguns and I'm not afraid to use them."

We put our diving equipment in a corner of the room and approached the door, Fats in the lead. We were almost close enough to see what was in the jar when it began to roll away from us and disappeared down the long, dark corridor. We could hear it tumbling down the path and we hurried in pursuit.

I turned on my flashlight and saw this was a straight corridor with walls of white jade. Two trenches ran along the base of each side. At the end of the hallway was a door which was flanked by two smaller ones. All three were wide open, showing us that someone had already gone inside. The jar was near the small door, unmoving, as

20. THE CORRIDOR OF DEATH

though it was waiting for us there.

This was peculiar, I thought, it was almost as though the jar had led us here; it had done everything but call out "Follow me." Did the creature inside have a mind? What was this thing and what was its purpose?

Fats was a step ahead of me. He tapped me on the shoulder and asked, "There are often traps set in places like this. Can you take a look and see if there are any suspicious signs?"

It was my turn to take the lead; I nodded and began to shine my flashlight over the walls and floor. The floor was littered with small bits of stone, which made me think there could be crossbow traps waiting for us to step in the wrong places and set them off. If Uncle Three had already been here, he probably had already dismantled any hazards that were set in place, but what if he hadn't? Cautiously I began leading the others down the long corridor.

I warned everyone to be aware of what they felt underfoot, any shifts or changes in the hard stone surface that they walked on, but I had little idea of what I was talking about. Detecting traps was an art form and I had almost no experience. I felt a surge of panic and tried to suppress it.

"Let's just take a break for a minute," Fats suggested as he saw me begin to hyperventilate.

"Shut up," I muttered. "If I stop paying attention for a second, we'll all die." Then I heard a thump and turned to see Ning staring at me in terror. One of the stones had caved under the weight of her foot.

There was a roar and a flash of white light as an arrow

flew past Ning's ear. Another had almost reached her chest but Ning leaped, turned in midair and caught the arrow in her hand. Her skill shocked me but there was no time to appreciate her hidden talents. The stones beneath my feet trembled and I yelled, "Duck! There are more hidden crossbows!"

A volley of white lights darted through the air and I ducked quickly to avoid arrows. As I bent down, I saw a little white creature crawl out of the jar and run through the small left-hand door. Before I could yell to my companions, there was a stabbing pain in my chest and I looked down to see two arrows buried in my skin.

20. THE CORRIDOR OF DEATH

CHAPTER TWENTY-ONE
TRANSFORMATIONS

There was nowhere to hide from the torrent of arrows that whizzed through the corridor. I caught a glimpse of Fats, whose back bristled with arrows like sticks of incense planted in an incense burner. For some reason, he seemed to be in no pain and I decided he had to be numbed by shock.

I stared at him thinking of novels I'd read about people shot with so many arrows they looked like porcupines. Was that the way we would look when people found our dead bodies in this tomb? And how crazy was it to die in another person's grave anyway! I cursed my Uncle Three more vehemently than I ever had before.

I felt myself jerked forward as someone grabbed me. I was relieved to see it was Ning, until I saw the cold and menacing look on her face. I pulled away from her but before I broke free, she kneed me in the groin and all of my strength was sapped by sheer agony.

She pushed me in front of her toward the large middle door. Arrows pierced my torso and I thought Shit! She's turned me into her human shield.

I'd already risked my life voluntarily for this woman once and that seemed to make her feel that I'd willingly serve as a sacrificial offering to save her again. But she overestimated my saintliness; I really wasn't the martyr she seemed to take me for. I tore myself from her hands and hurtled into the trench by the side of the corridor.

Without the protection of my body in front of her, Ning instantly faced a dozen arrows coming straight at her but she swiftly executed a pirouette to avoid them, then turned a hate-filled glare in my direction.

"What gives you the nerve to look at me like that?" I yelled and lunged toward her, but she leaped up onto the side of the wall, clinging to it like a lizard, and then jumped beyond my reach in one swift and agile motion. She turned toward me, disdainfully blew me a kiss, and walked unscathed through the middle doorway, swinging her hips insolently as she disappeared.

Enraged, all I could do was watch her go. Surrounding me was the swoosh of flying arrows followed by loud clanks as they struck the jade walls. They came in an unending barrage for at least five more minutes and then stopped.

Looking around for Fats, I saw a large round ball covered with arrows and knew it was him only because he was yelling obscenities. I hurried over to help him but he waved away my solicitude, saying, "Young Wu, what's wrong with these arrows? How can they go so deep but not hurt me? Would you pull them out please?"

I reached to yank an arrow from his back but I couldn't do it—I just didn't have the guts. As Fats cursed at me for being such a coward, Baldy emerged from where he had taken cover behind Fats and said, "Relax. Everything's going to be all right."

Fats and I stared at him; his voice had changed into one that we knew well. We gaped as Baldy stretched his body and with a few popping, clicking sounds, grew taller by several inches. He thrust both arms out into the air before him and with another pop, they lengthened by a couple of inches as well.

Impossible, I thought. I'd read about the art of bone contraction but never thought I'd ever see it done. It was an ancient kung fu skill used by grave robbers to get in and out of tight corners, allowing them to make their bones smaller so they could disappear down holes that were only large enough for a weasel to enter. It was a difficult skill to master; although my grandfather had written about this in his journal, he had never attained this talent himself.

But Baldy had more surprises in store for us. He sighed deeply, pulled at the back of his ears and to our horror ripped off his face, which was a lifelike latex mask. There standing before us was Poker-face.

Without saying a word, he moved his arms and shoulders about, as if he was relearning how to use them. We were speechless too until Fats shouted, "What in the hell are you up to? Are you deliberately jerking us around for the fun of it or is there some reason for this?"

Poker-face was silent as he helped Fats sit down. He gently grabbed one of the protruding arrows, gave it a hard twist, and pulled it from Fats's back, leaving only a small red bruise where it had been. There was no wound, no blood.

Taking courage from Poker-face's action, I grabbed an arrow embedded in my chest and it came out easily with no pain at all. I examined the arrowhead and found that it wasn't intended to be lethal. Once it hit its mark, the sharp end automatically retracted and was replaced with a metal clamp that tightly gripped the flesh of its victim without injury.

Poker-face looked at the floor of the corridor, which was carpeted with arrows, and at last spoke. "Ning stepped on that trap on purpose. Looks like she's not only a talented kung fu practitioner, she's a killer who planned to get rid of us all."

Fats grinned with relief and said, "If those goddamn arrows weren't harmless she would have been successful. Damn her, if I'd died with arrows all over my body like a hedgehog, people would remember me as a laughingstock forever."

I picked up one of the arrows to examine it again. "What's the point of a trap with bogus arrows?"

"I don't know," Poker-face answered, "but I knew these were harmless the minute the first one buried itself in your chest without stopping you, let alone wounding you. Maybe whoever built this tomb wanted to warn off intruders without killing them."

He didn't sound convincing but there was no time to debate the topic. "Ning's already on her way to the main tomb," I told him. "We can't let her slip in, grab everything there, and get away. Let's find that bitch now!"

I started for the door but Poker-face pulled me back. "Don't rush off without thinking. Whatever was in that jar signaled for us to take the door on the left. There was a reason for that. We're in its territory and we need to pay attention to its instructions."

"Damn it," I yelled at him, "if we don't follow Ning out the middle door, when she comes back this way to make her escape, we'll never find her."

"No problem," Fats assured me. "First we'll go back into the ear chamber and hide all the diving gear. She'll never make it out of here and get back up to the boat without an oxygen tank."

"That's brilliant," I agreed. "Why in hell didn't I think of that?" We rushed back to the spot where we'd left our equipment and stopped dead in our tracks. Everything was gone.

CHAPTER TWENTY-TWO
AN ELEVATOR

We stood staring at the empty space that just might be our death warrant. Who could have removed our oxygen tanks and other equipment? And how did the thief take them without our noticing? There was only one way out of the ear chamber, and even with all of the arrows flying around we would have noticed some stranger hauling away our oxygen supply.

"Could there be another zombie in here—a full-size one?" Fats asked nobody in particular. I waved my hand dismissively. This was no time to start babbling about hypothetical zombies. What were we going to do without our diving equipment? That was the question.

"Let's look around," Fats suggested. "Even if we don't find our stuff, we might find some clue as to who took it away and where it might have gone."

We rummaged around and the more we looked, the more disoriented I felt; everything seemed off-kilter in this room. "Shit," Fats yelled. "We've never been in this room before!"

His flashlight was shining into a far corner of the room where there had been nothing earlier, but which now held a column elaborately carved with exotic birds and animals. When we looked in the other three corners, we found an identical pillar in each one. We weren't in the room where we had left our equipment, that was certain.

"Look," Poker-face observed, "the small coffin is gone too and all of the burial porcelain is different from what we saw before. And look up."

When we raised our heads, we saw that the map painted with fifty stars had been replaced with two intertwining and menacing serpents that covered the entire ceiling.

"What happened? Did we come in through the wrong door?" I asked.

"How is that possible?" Fats argued. "There's only one way into this room—you know that. This is definitely the place where we entered the corridor."

Dazed, I realized we were in the same situation as Uncle Three when he awoke from his nap in a strange room. I was the only one who had all the facts; I should have known this might happen and ought to have prepared for it.

"You must have come across this kind of thing before in a tomb," Fats looked at me with hope in his eyes. "What did you do in your past experience?'

"It's time to come clean with you guys." I could barely speak, I was so choked with shame. "This is only my second time ever in a tomb. I don't know a damn thing about any of this—you can't count on me to clear up this mess."

"Young comrade, don't joke around like that." Fats looked amused. "You had me frightened for a minute there. I know you'll find the solution to our dilemma."

22. AN ELEVATOR

I tried to smile but it was a crooked grimace instead. "This is all so weird that not even an expert could figure this out. Not even my uncle." I paused, wondering how much of Uncle Three's story I should tell my companions. Besides, Poker-face or Zhang Qilin had been in that tomb twenty years ago and that still had me freaked out. I didn't know what he was up to or whether he could be trusted, so I decided to give a carefully edited version of my uncle's story.

When I finished, Fats shouted, "Damn you. By keeping this from us, you've led us into a state of being half-alive and nearly dead." Poker-face grabbed my arm, demanding, "What did your uncle say when you last saw him, when he ran off down the hallway of your hotel? Tell us again!"

"He said just one word—'elevator,'" I answered, and Poker-face smiled, saying, "So that's the trick."

CHAPTER TWENTY-THREE
SOLVING THE MYSTERY

"The strange thing is," Poker-face continued, "how simple this trick really is; it takes experience to figure it out, which is why your uncle just realized what it was twenty years after he fell for it."

"Spit it out," Fats interrupted. "I'm so eager to know that my kidneys ache."

"Here's an example," Poker-face told us. "Say there's a two-story building with only one room on each floor. While you're in the room on the second floor, I build another floor below the first-story without your knowledge. So when you come out of the second-story room, you are actually leaving the third floor and the first floor has become the second floor—but you still think there are only two floors."

Fats looked more confused than ever but I understood it at once; this really was a cheap trick. I had studied architecture in college and felt humiliated that I hadn't figured this out on my own. And after I explained it carefully to Fats, he agreed it was a logical, reasonable answer to the mystery.

Poker-face still looked troubled and muttered, "But there's a big difference between your uncle's experience and our own. He was sleeping in a room and didn't walk out of it as we did. No matter how the floors moved, he should still have been in the same place. What's more, ear chambers are called that for a good reason. There are always two of them that are symmetrical and across from each other. Where's the other chamber that matches this one?"

We walked back into the corridor and examined the wall on the opposite end; it was made of white jade with no apparent door within it. Poker-face ran his two abnormally long and sensitive fingers over the marble surface and found nothing.

Fats yawned. "Forget the other chamber. Even if we do find it, we'll still die. We need to find our oxygen tanks as well as our way out of here."

He made a certain amount of brutal sense, as usual. I began to wonder how my uncle made it safely out of here twice. Did he manage to find an escape route that eluded us now? Did he somehow dig his way up to the seabed?

I ransacked my memory for architectural principles, trying to figure out how this underwater tomb had been designed and what might possibly be above its ceiling. Since it was an airtight structure, I figured the bricks we had seen were sealed with cement and then wooden boards were placed on top of that with layers and layers of sealing wax. It would then be topped with more cement.

Once I arrived at this point, my brain sparked. "Listen, I have a plan," I announced to Fats and Poker-face. "I estimate we're about thirty feet below the bed of the sea. For this trick to work, the tomb must be very tall, with its top close to the seabed. I'm sure we can dig up to the top of the tomb and get out that way, especially if we do it during low tide."

"And what tools do we use for this to get through the layer of bricks," Fats asked sarcastically, "our hands?"

"You really don't have a clue, do you, Fathead. Most of the bricks used in underwater tombs are hollow. All we need are some metal objects to pound against the bricks and we'll come up with an opening."

"All right! Let's look for tools," Fats exclaimed. "Maybe we can find some big bronze objects somewhere in the main tomb."

"It might work," Poker-face muttered, "but it's a long time before low tide hits and I don't know how long it will be before we use up all the air in this place."

"Who cares about the tide, low or high? Let's find something to move these damn bricks," Fats yelped. "I'm not going to wait around and suffocate to death—I'd rather find a zombie and tell it to enjoy the meal."

I didn't tell him that if we didn't wait for the tide to turn, the water above us would be quite deep and would rush into the tomb as soon as we made an opening. Why dampen his spirits?

We walked back into the corridor and stopped in our tracks. In front of us was an open door and through it we could see a gold coffin made of nanmu wood.

CHAPTER TWENTY-FOUR
OPENING THE COFFIN

We weren't wildly surprised now that we knew what the trick was—the elevator had brought this room up silently as we were talking. What stunned us all was what the coffin was made of. The amount of nanmu logs that had been used to build this coffin was worth more than a piece of silver the size of a man. But why was something this valuable placed in an ear chamber? If the ear chamber held this, then the main tomb probably contained a coffin made of solid gold.

Who could fathom the logic of whoever had constructed this tomb? The place defied all common sense. Not only was its Feng Shui and placement disturbed and chaotic, but many ingenious traps had been set everywhere in the tomb. Yet they took no lives. What had the creator of this place been thinking?

The average grave robber's hands would feel uncontrollably itchy at the sight of a coffin, especially one like this which was bound to be filled with treasures. Fats's eyes were bulging with greed and I smiled, asking "What? Once you see the coffin you don't care about staying alive anymore? Are you dying to go ahead and take out a few pieces of treasure?"

I was being sarcastic, but he replied quite seriously. "I am a man of high conscience and I know what our main task is at present. We have to find tools so we can dig our way out of here through the ceiling of this place. Don't you forget that! We can always come back afterward and take a few things for posterity."

Amused by the rapacious yearning on his face that contrasted weirdly with his noble words, I said, "Who knows if this door will still be here when you come back? It could change again, and it probably will."

Poker-face waved at us and whispered, "Don't say another word." His face was so solemn and earnest that I immediately shut up. He pulled out his gun as he muttered, "This is no ordinary coffin. It's a corpse incubator."

I looked at him questioningly, but without explanation he walked into the ear chamber where the coffin lay. Fats rapidly abandoned his newfound moral outlook and eagerly followed. I looked around the corridor, realizing it would be too eerie to stay in the darkness alone, and ran to catch up with the others.

This chamber looked exactly the same as the one we just left, with two serpents embossed on the ceiling as well as a circular opening in the middle of the floor. However, the porcelain burial vessels were replaced by the gigantic coffin sitting three feet away from the wall.

Poker-face took out a knife and inserted it into the crevices of the coffin, slowly moving it as if looking for some sort of trap. Fats thought he was preparing to open the coffin, and yelled, "Take it easy! I thought you were an ethical sort of guy, so how come you don't care about your life now that you've seen the coffin?" Then he took out a candle and went over to the corner to light it.

"God damn you," I cursed. "We already have so little air in here, and now you're off lighting candles to use it up even faster? Do you want us all to die?"

Fats snapped back, "How much air can you lose by burning just one candle? At the worst I'll breathe one or two fewer lungfuls," and he ignited the lighter in his hand. As soon as the flame appeared, we saw a shadow in the corner of the room. Fats was usually daring but what he saw made him fall flat on his butt. I turned on my flashlight and shivered.

In the corner was a dry and shriveled cat in a mummified state. The eye sockets in its oversized head stared straight at Fats, and its jaw hung open, exposing a row of fangs. It had lost most of its skin and looked horrible.

Seeing that it was only a dead cat, Fats muttered something obscene, kicked it aside, lit his candle, and walked up to the coffin. We need to be careful, I thought, everything here goes against all the rules. If this keeps up, who knows what we'll find when we get to the main chamber?

Poker-face had already located the coffin's lock and was carefully working away at it. We heard a click, the lid of the coffin shot up into the air, and out poured a flood of black water. It looked disgusting and menacing but Fats didn't care. Pushing the coffin cover aside, he screamed, "Holy shit, there are so many zombies in this thing!"

CHAPTER TWENTY-FIVE
A CLUMP OF CORPSES

Once the coffin lid was opened, a stench like rotting fish filled the chamber. Holding my breath, I went over and looked down. The coffin was full of black water with a steamy mist coiling up from it. Inside I could vaguely make out so many limbs intertwined that it was impossible to determine how many corpses were there. The arms and legs were covered with wax and stuck together to form one huge and monstrous dead body. In less than a minute, I counted twelve hands.

Poker-face frowned at the sight, but his expression was already more relaxed than it had been a moment ago. His gun hung down by his side so I knew as horrible as this thing was, it wasn't dangerous. Why, I wondered, had he been so nervous when he entered this chamber?

Gold nails had been hammered in rows from the top to the bottom of the coffin every few feet; they were underwater so it was impossible to tell if they were pure gold or only plated. An object was visible beneath the corpse; Fats directed his flashlight along it inch by inch. It seemed to be a stone tablet engraved with text.

In the dead hands and lying around the arms and legs were objects made of jade and ivory, all very precious and very portable. I could tell Fats was dying to grab as many of them as he could but the corpses were too disgusting for even him to approach. Besides, it was completely wrong for a grave robber to reach into a coffin that contained a layer of human oil—even for one as crude and depraved as Fats. He pondered for a bit, found no solution, and turned his attention to the corpse instead. "This is too damn pathetic. Whoever owned this tomb was a barbaric bastard—how could he be so wicked as to put these people in here? He deserves to have us loot his grave."

The contents of the coffin confused me and harrowed my nerves; I couldn't take another look. "How come this coffin is so disgusting?"

Fats laughed at me. "Young comrade, have you gone nuts? Do you know anyone who would bury themselves like a twist of fried dough? This was obviously a live burial. These people were piled together, then they suffocated when a liquid drug was poured into the coffin. This is called a corpse incubator coffin."

When I heard him say fried dough, my throat suddenly convulsed. I was so hungry but when Fats described the corpse as a giant fried doughnut, I felt so sick I almost threw up my liver and kidneys too. But since it sounded as if he knew something about these dead people and why they were as we found them, I pulled myself together and asked for the details.

Delighted to have an audience, Fats was prepared to show off. "What! You don't know about this? You're like a child who never had a mother! All right, I'll tell you. It's a long story. I was at the lofty peaks of Mount Changbai..."

I knew how he rambled on and on when he started this sort of irrelevant nonsense and cut in quickly, "Stop bullshitting me; we don't have time for that. What the hell does corpse incubation have to do with Mount Changbai? If you don't know anything about this, then stop feeding me this garbage!"

Fats couldn't stand being provoked. He narrowed his eyes and said, "Who says I don't know anything about it? I just wanted to give you the bigger picture. If you don't want to hear it, then forget it. This is called a corpse incubator coffin. It's a branch of studies in Feng Shui. It's generally placed in the mountains. The existence of this coffin means in this tomb there are two excellent coffin placement spots in the Feng Shui sense. If a coffin is placed in a spot other than the two I just mentioned, then that would aggravate and attract demonic spirits due to the aura assembled in the sea valley. So a corpse incubator was placed here, and blood relatives of the grave owner were put in it, so they would be buried together. This coffin has to be an exact replica of the one in the main chamber. You get it?"

Fats spoke as though he had memorized this information without understanding any of it, and I only grasped half of what he told me. "There are so many people in there," I stammered. "Are they all—"

"Yes, damn it," Fats yelled, "that's exactly what I meant! This guy probably stuffed his entire damn family in there. It's appalling!"

"But why would he do that? The selection of a good Feng Shui position was for the sake of future generations in the first place. If he buried his entire family why worry about the Feng Shui?"

"So now you believe me," Fats gloated. "Have you ever met a wealthy man who was that stupid? He probably found some poor nephews on his wife's side to be buried with him. There are many things like this in tombs of the Ming dynasty. I have seen plenty of them, but never anything as big as this."

I looked at the body parts and began to think of the scene when this coffin had been interred. Grandfather had once told me that of all things, the hearts of men were the most unpredictable. These people's lives had counted as nothing and were taken from them because of a reason with no factual basis.

Now that the coffin lid was open, I reckoned there was no way the fat guy would so ignore the treasure inside. He shook his head and said, "Look how pitiful these people are. Why don't we go back to the other chamber, grab a few jars and scoop out the water? It's bad luck to leave water in a coffin."

I saw through his charity to his underlying motive and said, "Look at your hungry face. I know you just want to take out your loot. Why don't you calm down and stay put? There'll be plenty of things for you to take later at the offering platform in the main tomb."

Fats turned red. "Damn it. Do you really think I'm that kind of guy?"

Tired of his nonsense, I said, "Now is not the time for this. If we don't get out and if we suffocate in here, we won't even have a coffin after we die. No one will come and pity us."

Poker-face had been staring at the pile of corpses for a long time. Suddenly, he seemed to see something more and inhaled sharply. He was usually very calm so when he became nervous it was time to worry. I reached for the gun on my belt. He stared into the coffin, turned, and said, "There is only one body in here."

CHAPTER TWENTY-SIX
PORCELAIN PAINTING

I had just managed to understand what Fats was talking about and now Poker-face was saying something completely different, with no head or tail to his words. "What's going on?" I asked.

He pointed to the coffin and said, "Look carefully at the heads and see if you can tell the difference between them."

There were six heads of different sizes hanging on the body trunk like a bunch of grapes. Other than feeling nauseous, I had no other insight about them and shook my head, trying not to puke. "Look again, but more carefully," Poker-face told me. I squinted hard and finally saw what he meant.

Of the six heads, only the one on the top of the trunk had features or even a face. The others weren't even shaped like skulls; they looked like giant tumors that had grown on the body.

I understood. Following Poker-face's train of thought, I looked and saw that the joints of each hand seemed to be connected to the body trunk, which was severely twisted as if it had been laundered in a heavy-duty washing machine. The black water warped my vision, so on the surface it looked as if a number of bodies had been twisted together.

The more I looked, the more confused I became. I still had some reservations about Poker-face's theory. If the coffin indeed held a rare, deformed beast with twelve limbs, then what was its true origin and identity? How could a monster have been nurtured to become so enormous?

Fats spat and said, "Shit, how could this be a man? It's practically an insect!"

Although his remark was apt, it seemed rather cruel. "We can't see it clearly through the water," I protested. "It may be too soon to draw a conclusion. Logically speaking, this sort of severe deformity was considered evil. Its parents would have killed it the minute it was born. There was no way it would have grown up to be this size."

"Things aren't always absolute," Poker-face remarked.

I shook my head, still unconvinced that what he had said was true. "It's actually very simple to find out," Fats said. "Why don't we do what I said, get a few jars from next door and scoop out this water. Then we can have a better look and we can examine the stone tablet the monster is lying on. Who knows what we'll learn from that?"

I became enthusiastic at the thought of finding some text. Ever since we had entered the tomb, there had been nothing written anywhere and I longed for some information about the owner of this grave. If there were words on the stone tablet, what we might learn from it could help us all.

Without another word, Fats and I returned to the room on the opposite side of the corridor. We picked up three porcelain bowls with handles, which would be million-dollar treasures in the outside world. Out of professional habit, I began to examine the blue and white porcelain glaze as I picked up the bowl and was stunned. I had no idea that the pattern on the glaze told a story.

My mind had been preoccupied with the fate of my Uncle Three and so I didn't carefully study these vessels when I first saw them. Now as I looked at the porcelain bowl, I immediately thought of something that I should have realized before.

When my uncle and the archaeology students had first entered this tomb, Uncle Three only took a cursory glance at these things and then fell asleep. But the others were different. Since it was their first time in an ancient tomb, they were very excited. It was only natural they would carefully study this chinaware. Could the clue to their disappearance be found in the pictures on the porcelain?

I hurriedly picked up a few more bowls and looked at them carefully. On them was drawn the story of a group of people participating in a civil engineering project. Some repaired stonework, some transported logs, and others put up wooden beams. The project in the picture was carefully shown in chronological order on the long line of burial vessels. As I perused each one in turn, Fats grew impatient and said, "Is it that difficult to choose a jar? Stop being so picky. Just get one that fits your hands."

I paid no attention to him; I ducked down and studied each vessel one by one as I crawled on. I didn't stop until I reached the octagonal vase, which was the last in the row. On it was a powerful and extravagant scenario. That was all; I felt sure there must be more recorded on other porcelain vessels in other rooms.

I was so excited it was hard to breathe. Although I could not be definite about what the project was that the people were building, I could tell from the simple paintings that the project was vast, its size comparable to that of the Forbidden City. However, its design didn't look like the architecture style of the Central Plains. I really could not figure where the devil in China such an enormous structure had been built.

I refocused, ready to tell Fats about my amazing discovery. I turned, but saw only darkness behind me. The son of a bitch had run out on me.

That asshole, he knew I hated to be alone in places like this, but he didn't even have the decency to tell me he was taking off. I picked up a bowl at random, stood up, and hurried back to the ear chamber on the other side. Once I entered the corridor, I stopped dead. The door was gone; once again there was only the white jade wall.

I knew this was just the trap doing its usual trick, but I hadn't expected it to operate so rapidly. I started to panic. I didn't want to have to wait alone in a dark ancient tomb ever again.

I calmed down and tried to reassure myself. All I had to do was wait patiently. This elevator was fast and frequent; I estimated the door would inevitably reappear in just a few more minutes.

But without Fats, the tomb was frighteningly quiet. My heartbeat was the only sound I could hear and it grew louder by the second. It was outrageously dark. A minute was like an eon in this place. It was really impossible for me to practice patience any longer.

26. PORCELAIN PAINTING

Taking a deep breath, I pointed my flashlight into the dark doorway before me. I could see nothing except what lurked in my own imagination and I was positive that something was looking at me from the door.

My saliva turned to sand in my mouth and I knew I had to do something or I'd go crazy from fear. Lowering my head, I walked back toward the room I had just left, wanting to be sure I'd examined every porcelain vessel. As I got closer, I heard a hideous cry coming from the room I approached. Pointing my flashlight into the doorway, I saw a giant sea monkey climbing out of the circular opening in the middle of the room, its scaly face glaring in my direction.

I ran into the corridor, and racing down it with my eyes shut, I tripped over a jar and fell. Glancing behind me, I saw only two glowing green eyes moving swiftly into the hallway and coming straight at me.

I gritted my teeth, picked up the jar, and threw it. The sea monkey reacted quickly. Seeing that I had a weapon, it did not rush over blindly but changed course and jumped up to the ceiling of the corridor. I took the opportunity to slip into the door at my left and swiftly slammed it shut.

There was an automated stone bolt near the threshold. As soon as I closed the door, the bolt bounced up into place and I was safe. The sea monkey screamed and roared and pounded in its efforts to get at me, but I knew the door was made of stone and could not be broken through by flesh and blood.

After banging on the door without success, the sea monkey decided to slide in through the cracks between the door and the wall. I saw him rubbing his head along that space, and I became enraged. I picked up a speargun, aimed it at the door crack, and fired the missile. I didn't know where it landed, but I heard the sea monkey shriek and jump back from the door.

I quickly reloaded my gun and then turned on both my flashlight and searchlight to take a look at where I might be. In a second, the entire room was illuminated. Once I took it all in, I was shocked. I was in a huge circular chamber with a huge pool in the middle. My feet stood exactly at the edge of the pool. One more step and I would have fallen in.

Something was floating in the middle of the pool, and judging by what was carved on its surface, I could tell it was certainly a coffin. I smiled. The owner of this grave was quite clever and made his own coffin to look like a tub. He must have been very fond of baths when he was alive.

I pointed the flashlight into the water. The bottom of the pool was invisible so I had no idea of how deep it was— perhaps it went all the way to the bottom of this tomb. As I peered into it, I began to feel a maddening itch at the back of my neck.

26. PORCELAIN PAINTING

CHAPTER TWENTY-SEVEN
THE TOMB BUILDER

Touching the back of my neck, I realized I itched in the spots where I'd been struck by the lotus arrows, where their hooks had clasped onto my skin. Although they hadn't hurt me, they had still scraped away some of my skin, and my neck itched as sweat ran into the lacerations.

A few other spots where the arrows hit my body became irritated but I had no time to consider the subtleties of these physical sensations. There was a chamber to explore and it would take all of my concentration.

I didn't know much about the underground tombs inhabited by commoners during the Ming dynasty. I had only studied about the tombs of noblemen and didn't know what differences there were between the two. I could only fumble about, comparing what lay before me with what I already knew.

Based on my knowledge, I was standing now in the left Identical Hall. The room facing me was the right Identical Hall. Both halls were exactly the same in every detail, so it was quite probable that there would be another white marble coffin platform in the right hall. The platform's surface was tiled with transparent glass bricks. Usually there was a rectangular opening in the middle of the platform that filled with yellowish brown silt called the "gold well," but I saw nothing like that here, only the huge pool.

This was only one of the unusual features of this chamber. The other was the door that separated the two halls. It should have led to the back chamber, which was where the coffin ought to be. But here the coffin had been placed in the left Identical Hall. Even more peculiar was that it had been made in the shape of a bathtub. This type of coffin was a product of the Warring States Period, and wasn't made during the Ming dynasty.

This made me think of the Bronze Fish with Snake Brows I took from the tomb of the Ruler of Dead Soldiers, another of which also was found here. Now here was a coffin from the same period as the tomb where I found the fish. Was there some connection between these two places or was this only a coincidence?

My mind was as confused as a bunch of tangled noodles and I decided to stop thinking for a while. I had walked around the pool and was back at the door where I had hurled the porcelain jar at the sea monkey. I picked it up and began to examine the painting that ornamented it. On it was a man in the dress of the Ming dynasty standing on a hill above a construction site with several people dressed in official garb. It looked as though they were inspecting a building project.

Judging from this picture, I decided that the owner of this tomb wasn't someone from the imperial family or the aristocracy but probably a craftsman or an architect. Only that kind of person would have the capability and the knowledge to build a tomb like this one. Even if an ordinary man had been able to conceive of this place, he would never have had the training and skill to make his dream come true.

In addition, there weren't many able artisans at this time in the Ming dynasty. Considering the scale and size of the tomb, the owner must been a man of prominent position, someone with good social standing. Not only must he have had the qualifications to be in charge of a project that was as vast as any Ming palace, but it was essential that he understood Feng Shui and other arcane disciplines. This narrowed down the possibilities and after a few minutes, a name popped into my head—Wang Canghai.

This man was well known for being unique and mysterious. His accomplishments in Feng Shui were unrivaled, and so he had been appointed directly to take part in the construction of several Ming palaces. He had also designed a few of China's metropolises, and one word from his mouth was enough to ensure that other cities in the empire would disappear. I had read in ancient texts that he had written a book on Feng Shui that was brilliant, a glimpse of one of the most remarkable minds that ever lived. Unfortunately, his descendants had only reproduced a few copies of this treasure and all of these had been lost.

According to legend, the fabulous undersea tomb of Shen Manzo had been designed by Wang Canghai. It would have been an easy matter for this man to construct a tomb of the same design for himself.

I thought my theory made a lot of sense—I just needed some text to back it up, but so far there were no written inscriptions. Was the owner of this tomb really the genius Wang Canghai, or was he some illiterate yokel with too much money?

A noise coming from the pool drew me from my speculations and I quickly turned my flashlight in that direction. Bubbles of different sizes rose to the surface, coming and going with no regular pattern, as though something was moving in this bottomless abyss of water.

Alarmed, I picked up my gun and stared at the bubbles with a large amount of apprehension. Something shining and white came out of the water, rolled next to the wall, and began to gasp for air. I was ecstatic—it was Fats!

He had taken off his shirt, and his naked, flabby stomach wobbled as it growled with hunger. He saw me as he panted, waved, and stuttered, "Damn—damn it—I—almost—suff—suffocated."

Before I could ask him what had happened to him, another man came out of the water and lay near my feet. It was Poker-face. He was also shirtless and I could see that his qilin tattoo had disappeared.

Whatever had occurred was obviously less draining for him than it had been for Fats. He looked up, took a deep breath, saw me, and asked, "Is this the left Identical Hall or the right?"

When I told him it was the left, he looked relieved and sat down, clasping his wrist. On it I could see a black scratch from what was obviously a claw and suddenly felt a premonition of danger and doom.

It took a long time before Fats's breathing returned to normal, as he clutched his stomach and gasped for air. "How did you get to this place?" I asked. Fats gagged up a glob of mucus and then said, "Never mind that.

Thank God you weren't there, it almost scared the shit out of me. Luckily there was a hole under the stone tablet in that coffin that led us here. Otherwise, we would have died in that place!"

Baffled, I asked, "What was so terrifying?"

"Fuck me, I can't even describe it myself," Fats replied. "In one sentence—there was some goddamn thing in the stomach of that corpse cluster."

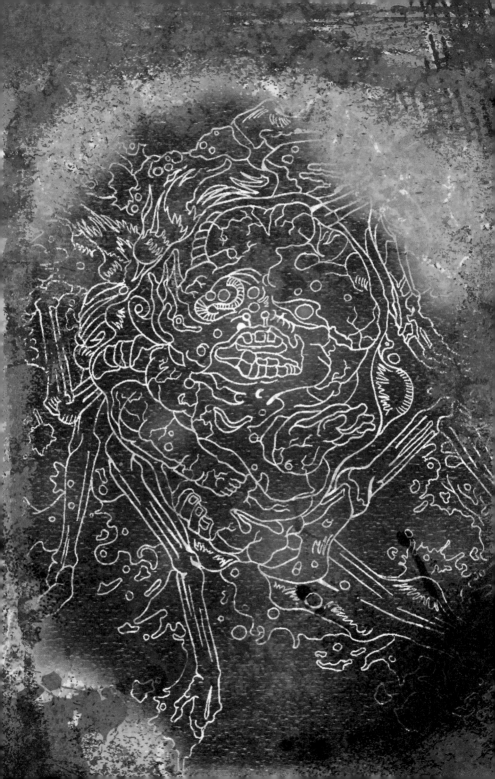

CHAPTER TWENTY-EIGHT
THE BABY

Fats coughed and spat a few more times. "Don't leave me hanging—tell me, damn it," I said, and he glared at me.

"At least you can breathe a little while you're hanging. Give me a minute. This happened so fast that I can't tell you everything all at once. Let me get my thoughts together here."

His face was grey and his voice squeaked as though he still had water in his lungs. I pounded his back hard, and he bent over, vomiting up black fluid. "Okay, all right, that's enough," he choked. "I'll be dead if you keep smacking me like that."

"Hurry up and tell me what happened to you guys."

He blew his nose and gave me a brief account of what they had gone through. His story was a bit incoherent but he gave me the general idea and that was more than enough to make me feel uneasy.

While I was staring blankly at the porcelain vessels in the room at the end of the corridor, Fats had called me a few times, urging me to hurry up, but I was preoccupied and didn't hear him. My lack of response and undoubtedly his obsession with the valuable jade and ivory in the other chamber made him decide to run back alone. He reasoned that I'd come back on my own after choosing my bowl. After all, the two rooms were only five or six steps away from each other—what could go wrong?

What happened next distracted him so completely that he forgot I existed.

Fats returned to the coffin and he and Poker-face began to scoop out the water. Soon the corpse floated above the water level and Fats almost puked when he got a good look at it. The tumors that he had previously thought were heads were actually massive, corpulent female breasts, so pendulous that they hung down on the twisted torso. Fats was gobstruck; he'd never thought that the corpse could be a woman.

Since there were twelve arms, there should be twelve breasts but on the front of the body there were only five. Could the others be on the back? He and Poker-face thought this over as they tried to figure out how to lift the body out of the coffin.

In their first attempt to bring up the corpse, Fats used his spearguns as hooks to grab onto the body. But its flesh was too soft, almost entirely covered with wax, and so satiny there was no spot that could be grasped. They put on gloves and tried to grip it, but this was even more impossible. The body was as slippery as a bar of soap and when touched it exuded an oil that was thoroughly revolting.

Finally, Poker-face came up with a solution. They took off their shirts, wrapping one around the body's head and the other around the feet. With a gun serving as their carrying pole, they lifted up the body and put the dead woman on the ground.

28. THE BABY

Under the bright light of the lamp, they could see the corpse rapidly become black and dry, which allowed them a closer examination. Her other breasts had been cut off, leaving a few scars the size of bowls on both sides of her body, which was not twisted as they had thought but was distorted by gigantic mounds of flab.

At first they chalked up the corpse's mammoth stomach to her immense amount of body fat, but now they could clearly see that at the time of her death she was carrying a child—her stomach bore a whole other universe within its rolls of flesh.

After the corpse was lifted from the coffin, they could see the stone tablet clearly. Poker-face identified it as a coffin weight, put there so that the coffin would not float up to the water's surface if the airtight seal of the tomb was broken.

Carved on its rough surface was a long line of text and when Fats couldn't decipher it, he finally remembered me. It was only then that my two companions realized that the door that would take them out to the corridor had disappeared.

"My God, you and I are dead men," Fats howled to Poker-face, giving no thought to me, of course.

"Don't get hysterical," Poker-face told him. "You know the door will reappear. Stop worrying and help me finish the job we have here."

Calmed down by Poker-face's equanimity, Fats began to help him remove the tablet. Not only was it very heavy, but someone had poured pine sap all around it which glued it firmly to the bottom of the coffin.

"Let's check this out," Fats said, and knocking on the top of the tablet, he discovered that beneath it was a hollow space. Lighting matches, they melted away the pine sap and lifted the tablet, exposing a large hole.

Now Fats was uneducated and without any culture whatsoever, but he made up for those deficiencies with years of experience in his trade. "Holy shit," he announced. "This wasn't put here by the tomb's builder. This is a grave robbers' tunnel.

"This is a huge discovery," he continued. "The positioning of this tunnel alone is unparalleled anywhere else in the world of grave robbing. It's been dug directly to the bottom of the coffin. If not for the coffin-weight blocking the way, the corpse would probably have fallen through the hole long ago. And the most bizarre thing is this is an undersea tomb, so what method was used to dig the robbers' tunnel?"

Both he and Poker-face grew quiet. Fats knew what he was talking about. Still he was no expert; he could narrow down possibilities but that was about as far as he could go. Thinking that the inscription carved on the tablet could be the key to the mystery, he copied it quickly onto a piece of paper and then heard Poker-face exclaim, "Shit!"

Looking up, Fats saw a small, feathery, white hand stretch from the belly of the corpse and grip Poker-face's left wrist. Quickly he grabbed his speargun and fired at the little hand. His aim was perfect and Poker-face broke free. He began to reload his gun but Poker-face shouted, "You can't kill this thing! Go!" and yanked him into the coffin toward the robbers' tunnel.

28. THE BABY

The last dregs of the coffin's oily liquid dripped down into the tunnel and Fats felt sick when he saw it. He was reluctant to enter until he turned and looked at the corpse. The skin on her belly was pulled so tight that it was transparent, and Fats could see the shape of a tiny face protruding from the dead woman's stomach. It looked as though it were trying desperately to come out into the world and Fats could see its crazed little eyes boring into his own. He tightened his jaw and crawled after Poker-face.

The tunnel had been dug in a sophisticated manner, by people who had carefully moved the bricks by breaking them in half. This created an arched brick beam at the top of the tunnel to prevent things falling down from above. This could only have been done by skilled craftsmen and probably took more than a few days' work to accomplish.

Fats began chasing Poker-face in a frenzy, with no idea of where either of them was going. After a few steps, the tunnel changed direction and tilted downward. There was water below and Fats saw a flashlight beaming through it. Thinking it had to be me, he plunged into the water. Poker-face was already there and together they swam to the end of the tunnel, where they found my pool. They floated to the surface, climbed out of the water, and found me aiming a speargun at them.

At this point I had to interrupt, "So all you saw was a hand."

"I wasn't afraid of that thing," Fats protested, "but when this guy ran from it, what could I do? You know he's the one with the power and when he runs, I follow. But tell me," and he turned to Poker-face, "just why did we run?

I saw the size of that thing and I could have disposed of a baby—no problem."

Poker-face touched his left wrist and said, "That baby was a white-feathered Drought Demon. You can only kill it by cutting off its head, and even then when it dies it will release a huge cloud of poison gas. We already have precious little oxygen to spare—it just wouldn't have been worth it."

I was amazed. The Drought Demon is a legendary evil spirit. If a zombie is nurtured for a long time, it will turn into this, people say. Ancient writings tell us that the Drought Demon is cruel and deadly and brings such severe aridity that the land will burst into flames. There were many stories about this creature and I never thought it truly existed.

What a dreadful place we've come to, I thought, and how will we ever get out of it? Why is the tunnel connected to this pool and not to an exit? Are there perhaps other tunnels going in different directions?

"When you were off without me, did you find any forks in the tunnel's pathways?" I asked the others.

Fats shook his head and my spirits sank. Since the tunnel was airtight, it must have been dug completely within the tomb with no outside entrance. Whoever dug it must have come into the tomb as we did, found no door in the ear chamber, and then dug a tunnel to the coffin with the stone tablet in it, then excavated his way to this pool. Could he possibly have dug his way into the main chamber, I asked myself and then was interrupted by Fats blurting, "Say, do you think the Drought Demon can swim?" He pointed to the pool. Its surface was covered with bubbles.

28. THE BABY

CHAPTER TWENTY-NINE
THE TABLET

Bubbles popped and then resumed their shapes as we stared at the water. It looked as though something or someone really big was breathing below the surface of the pool and we immediately went on full alert, guns poised, backs tight against the wall. The water looked as though it was in full boil for about five minutes and then stopped as a mysterious noise emerged from the depths of the pool.

The water level began to recede and a dozen little whirlpools appeared on the surface, with water splashing over the pool's edges as though a dozen toilets were being flushed simultaneously. The coffin spun about in the middle like a gyrating top and in a couple of minutes the pool was two or three feet lower than its original level.

I directed the beam of my flashlight into the water and saw on the inner walls of the pool there was a staircase, spiraling downward toward the bottom.

With a whoosh, the water drained away into the darkness and we could see that the walls of the pool were in the shape of a bowl, wide above, narrow below, and easily twenty feet deep. Mist swirled in steamlike clouds above the bottom and it was impossible to see what lay below us.

We still carried our underwater searchlights which might be able to pierce through the mist, I realized, and we all focused our beams into the vaporous curtain. Vaguely we could see that the bottom of the pool was a circular flat surface covered with bas-relief carvings and large holes, like drains, on the floor. We stared through flickering shadows of mist and Fats yelled, "Hey look! Is that a tablet in the middle of the pool's bottom?"

"Your eyes are like battery acid—they burn through everything. I can barely see what you're talking about," I replied.

"Who knows where this staircase goes? Let's have a look—maybe there are more tunnels," Fats shouted and raced down to the bottom of the pool, calling back, "Don't worry. I'm just going to take a look and if there's nothing worth our time, I'll be right back."

I knew he was too stubborn to stop; all I could do was watch him go and hope for the best. He walked about and then bent down as though he was examining something. Straightening back up, he shouted to us, "Fuck me, something's written in English down here!"

"What the hell are you talking about?" I yelled back. "How could there be English inscriptions in an ancient tomb? Are you sure you aren't looking at carvings of flowers, you ignorant bastard?"

Fats looked pissed off. "So what if I'm not a brilliant scholar like you? Maybe I can't read English but I know my ABCs. Stop badmouthing me and come down and see for yourself if you don't believe me—if you dare, you wimp."

"Read it to me," I taunted and he roared, "If I could read, why would I need your useless carcass hanging around? Get down here, damn you."

Sighing, I reluctantly made my way down the wet and slippery steps. Luckily they were strong, carved from granite, so I had no fear of them collapsing under my feet. With Poker-face close behind me, I approached the spot where Fats waited, pointing at the wall.

"Look at this and tell me if I wasn't correct. If this isn't English, I'll carry you out of the tomb on my back, every step of the way."

I looked at the letters chiseled on the stone wall. It was impossible to tell when they had been inscribed, a thousand years ago or last month. I suddenly thought of the students who came with my uncle twenty years before. Could they have written these words here while Uncle Three slept? Could their disappearance be connected with this weird pool?

Annoyed by my silence, Fats pounded me on the back and bellowed, "Come on, admit it, I'm right, aren't I?"

"Yes, I'm sorry. It's English."

Pleased with himself, Fats bragged, "I knew this was a fucked-up situation. How could we spend so much time down here without finding any real treasure? It was our Foreign Guests who beat us to the punch and took everything away with them, just as they've been doing since the Boxer Rebellion. Those bastards never leave anything for those of us who are Chinese and truly deserve the rewards of our own history."

I thought for a minute and told him, "You don't know for sure if foreigners were here; we Chinese can read and write English too and it's more efficient to use when carving in stone—it's much faster to write than our own language. Look, these letters are initials and I think they are a kind of message written in a hurry. Maybe it was during an emergency and someone wanted to leave information for his companions who would come later on."

"You could be right," Fats conceded. "What do you think they were doing down here? Do you think there might still be some valuable things left for us to find?"

I knew all too well where his mind was going and ignored him, but he kept rattling on. "What we have now is time. Let's go have a look. Maybe we'll find some things made of bronze or copper that we can use to dig our way out, as well as other things to make our lives better after we find our way back to dry land."

Just as I was about to tell Fats that I didn't give a damn about finding treasure to make my future blissful if it meant I'd give up my life to pay for it, Poker-face spoke.

"I think I've been in this place before."

CHAPTER THIRTY
AT THE BOTTOM OF THE POOL

"What are you talking about?" I asked, but he ignored me and raced off down the staircase. If I wanted answers, I knew I couldn't lose track of him and followed close behind through the barrier of thick fog. Fats ran past me, the glow of his flashlight a beacon in the misty darkness. And then both he and Poker-face vanished.

Shrouded in mist, my vision was as bad as an old man with cataracts; I could see no more than a foot ahead of me or behind me. It was almost worse than being totally blind. I was relieved to hear Fats shout, "I'm here at the bottom. You're close by. Come on down!"

I could hear the splashing of his footsteps and ran down to where the sound came from. My feet suddenly felt paralyzed by cold and in another second I was standing in water that reached halfway up my legs. I had reached the very bottom of the incompletely drained pool, surrounded by mist. Clutching at the nearby wall, I walked to where I figured Fats would be and then heard his voice. "Be careful of the drainage holes. They're big."

He was right. There were bowl-like recesses in the surface of the floor, and I stepped carefully to avoid breaking my ankle. A light shone toward me and there was Fats and his flashlight, guiding me to safety.

Shapes loomed out of the clouds of vapor and I stopped with a certain amount of caution, if not fear. "Don't dawdle, damn it. Come over here," Fats grumbled. He stood near what I could now see were four stone statues of monkeys, each one half the size of a man. They were crouched upon a pedestal, each turned in a different direction of the compass. All of them stood in prayer and I knew they were Sea-Calming Monkeys that were put in the bottoms of ponds or pools to ward off evil water-spirits.

The monkey statues were placed around a large vertical tablet, about six feet high. Standing beside it was Poker-face, examining it in deep concentration.

Walking over, I asked, "What's up? What do you remember?"

He pointed and I saw something written on the front of the tablet in tiny letters.

Fats ran up, asking, "What's there?"

"A few sentences that say the owner of this tomb built a heavenly palace and the door leading to it is in this tablet. For those people who share an affinity with this place, the door will open and will lead them into heaven."

Fats snorted. "And where the fuck is that door anyway?"

"This could almost be a Zen text, which can be interpreted differently by everyone who reads it," I explained. "It may not mean a literal door, only that a message here will lead us to an entrance."

"My ass," Fats cursed. "Where are the words you're talking about? I can't see a damn thing on that tablet."

I looked again and now the tablet was bare of any carving at all, just highly polished like a piece of jade. "Of course there's nothing there now. It said it was there only for those who shared an affinity with it. What affinity could there possibly be between you and heaven?"

Fats spat, bent down, and began groping about in the water. "I don't care if there's an affinity between me and heaven, just so long as there's an affinity between me and treasure. If there's anything here, I'm going to damn well find it."

I turned to look at Poker-face who was pale and sweaty. "Are you okay?" I asked him, but he stared silently at the tablet as though it had something to tell him, although as far as I could see, there was nothing on it anymore.

Fats let out a whoop. "Look what I found!" His dripping hand clutched a pair of diving goggles. "Somebody sure was here before we came."

"When Uncle Three came out of this tomb after his first trip, he was wearing no diving equipment. Maybe those were his. Is there anything else in there?"

In reply, Fats pulled out an oxygen tank. He tested it, but it was no longer functional and he tossed it back into the water. "Everything here seems to be worn-out and useless. What a bitch to come down here, risk our lives, and find nothing. I say let's get out of here now. The water could easily flood the pool again and then we'll be fucked even if we suddenly were able to fly."

"You're finally making some sense, Fat Man," I said and turned to grab Poker-face. He had disappeared and when I called, there was no answer.

30. AT THE BOTTOM OF THE POOL

"God damn this guy—he's like a ghost, vanishing and reappearing—pain in the ass," Fats observed, and for once I had no desire to argue with him. We searched and although the area we were confined to was small, the fog was thick. It took some time before we finally found him, squatting in a corner. His whole body screamed despair and his eyes looked like a dead man's.

As I came toward him, he looked at me and muttered as though it hurt his throat to speak. "What happened twenty years ago. I can remember it now. Listen and I will tell you everything…"

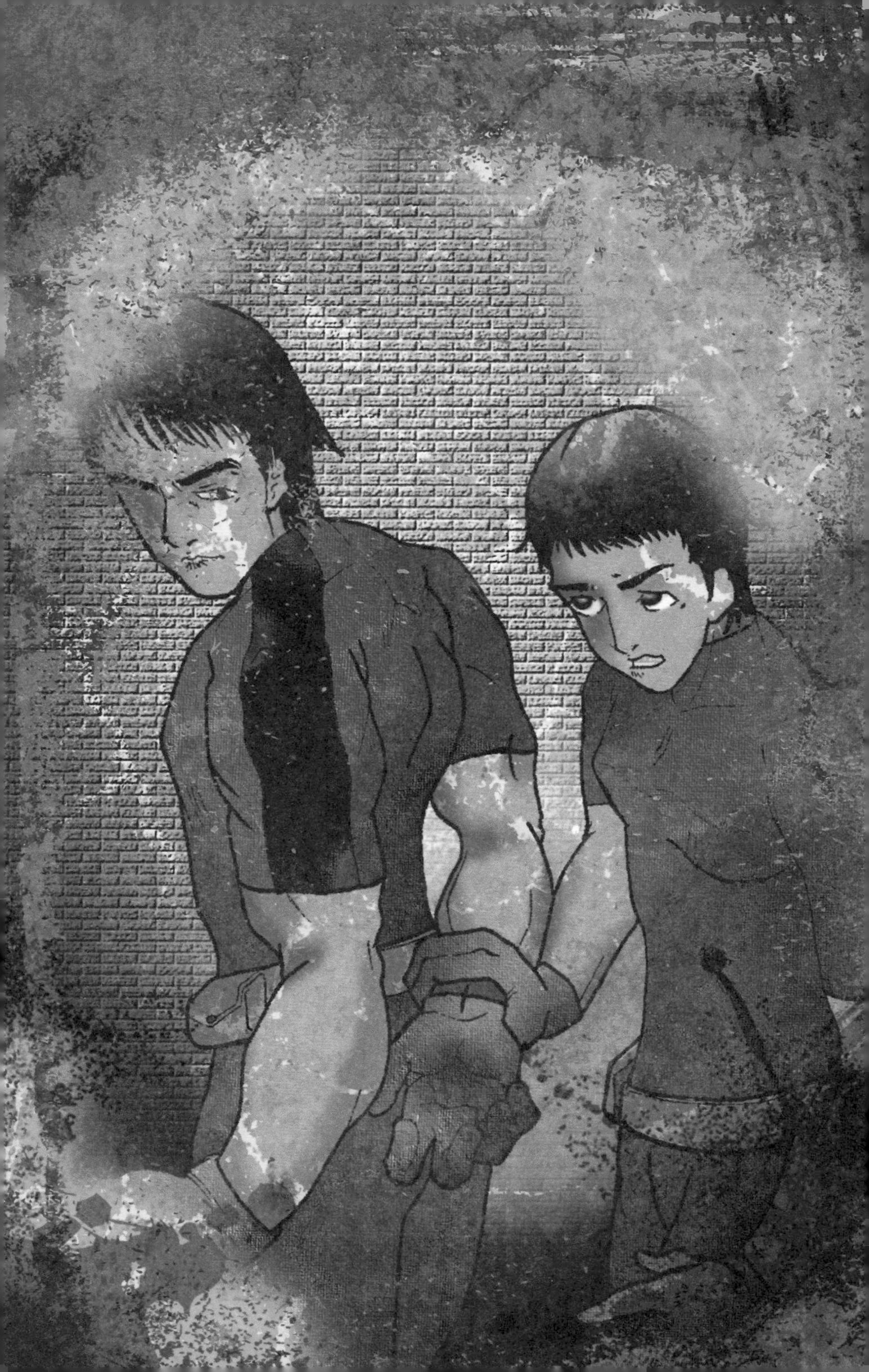

CHAPTER THIRTY-ONE
ZHANG QILIN'S STORY

Zhang Qilin sat quietly in the corner of the ear chamber, watching. His companions jostled each other to look at the blue and white porcelain objects on the floor as their captain snored with Wen-Jin sitting beside him. Although the chinaware did not appeal to him at all, everybody in his archaeological group was completely entranced by the patterns and images that they found painted on the vessels.

"Come here and look, everyone! I've found something very odd on this piece." It was Huo Ling, the youngest of the three girls on the team. She was the pampered daughter of high-level government officials, and she often made loud comments about nothing at all to gain attention. Because she was pretty, all of her male classmates were happy to drop everything at the sound of her voice, except for Zhang Qilin, who thought she was a complete pain in the neck.

He was the only person who didn't scurry over to examine the object that Huo Ling held in her hands. "This—I know what this is," one boy announced importantly. "It's a kiln number; it shows where the porcelain was made."

"You're wrong," another boy argued. "Kiln numbers from the Ming dynasty don't look like that. It's probably an inscription of the official title that was given to the grave owner."

"Inscriptions of government titles always have four characters. There's only one word here, and it's quite unusual. You're the one who's wrong," the first boy retorted. Their dispute became heated, and Huo Ling sighed with boredom. Why, she wondered, were boys so predictable?

Gazing about the room for a new diversion, she noticed Zhang Qilin in the corner, looking as bored as she was; the only one who had paid no attention to her now or at any other time, for that matter. Annoyed by his lack of interest, she walked to him and stuck the porcelain jar under his nose. Smiling in her most beguiling manner, she begged sweetly, "Young Zhang, help me please? Would you take a quick look and tell me what's written on here?'

Reluctantly, Zhang Qilin took a passing glance at what she held and then turned away. "I have no idea," he said in a flat tone that turned Huo Ling's face to stone. Stamping her tiny foot, she cried, "Don't ignore me. Look at this and tell me what this inscription means; it could be important, you know," and she pushed the jar into Zhang Qilin's hands.

He sighed with impatience as Huo Ling drew close to him and pointed out the characters that nobody could decipher. To his surprise, it did look as though it might be special; it was not, he knew, a kiln number.

Picking up another jar, he saw it had an inscription on its bottom as well, similar but not identical to the one

Huo Ling had found. I don't think these are simple burial objects, he thought, they carry some sort of information.

Huo Ling was watching him closely and saw his attention focus upon her discovery. At last I've made this wooden-headed dolt notice me, she thought proudly, and murmured softly, "Tell me, Young Zhang, what have I brought you that you like so much? I always knew we would finally find something we could talk about together." She moved her hands close to his as though she was safeguarding the jar that he held. It took long enough but I have him now, she gloated to herself.

Zhang Qilin brushed past her as though she had no importance at all and began to scrutinize piece after piece of the porcelain objects that covered the floor of the chamber. After examining a dozen of them, he found that each had a different inscription that changed in a regular pattern, like sequential numbers. Why, he wondered, and why had they so carefully been placed in order?

He looked closer and saw that the paintings on each piece of porcelain showed a sculptor carving a gigantic statue, instead of the typical scene of farmers in the fields or of flowers in a courtyard. Just as the inscriptions on the bottoms of the pieces changed, so did the pictures that were painted on them. As he looked at them in the order that they had been placed, he saw small, subtle changes in the work being done by the sculptor; slowly it became clear that each piece showed a part of a huge construction project. He walked to the end of the row of pieces and picked up the last object in line, a double-handled pot. Painted on it was a picture of the completed project.

It was a palace floating in the sky, enshrouded by mist and clouds. The men who had been depicted in other paintings as the builders were below on the ground, staring up at what they had created.

Zhang Qilin was certain that this was a discovery beyond all others—the painting on this small pot was certainly a picture of the Palace of Heaven, the creation of the Ming dynasty master, Wang Canghai. The legendary palace in the clouds often figured in ancient fables, but it was explained that by using a huge kite anchored with miles and miles of golden thread, Wang Canghai had created an illusion of a magnificent floating mansion to please the founding emperor of the Ming dynasty, Zhu Yuanzhang.

If the fables were true, then what was the meaning of the paintings he had just discovered? Didn't these pictures indicate that Wang Canghai had really built a palace perched above the clouds? Legend or paintings—which was real and which was a lie? Zhang Qilin began to feel confused.

He showed his companions what he had found and they all agreed that this was a discovery that could transform Chinese history. Huo Ling forgot her former pique and kissed him on the cheek, which gained the attention of every male in the chamber except for Uncle Three, who still snored in the corner, and Zhang Qilin, who was so deep in thought that he didn't even notice what had happened.

He pushed past her once again to go to Wen-Jin. "We need to go immediately to investigate the main chamber," he urged her. "I'm sure there are more clues to this discovery within the coffin there."

"No way. Absolutely no way are we going into the tomb," she objected. "We're not leaving this chamber until our captain wakes up to guide us."

There was no point in arguing with her, Zhang Qilin realized. He picked up his equipment and started toward the doorway without a word. Upset that he ignored her, Wen-Jin stepped forward quickly, ready to stop him with one of the kung fu moves she had perfected over the years.

She reached for his wrist in a move that was capable of bringing a man to his knees, shrieking for mercy. Zhang Qilin moved slightly and, for the first time ever, she missed her target. He smiled at her and said, "Don't worry. As you see, I can take care of myself."

"How?" Wen-Jin sputtered in embarrassment. "Young Zhang, you are notorious for your undisciplined and headstrong behavior, and now we're in a place where we might all die because of your impetuous nature. If you don't care about yourself, at least be considerate of your companions' safety."

Nodding, Zhang Qilin replied, "I'll certainly consider that. We'll discuss it in a minute, when I come back."

Furious, Wen-Jin grabbed his arm. "No. No matter what, you're not allowed to leave. We've already lost one person in this place. How will I explain it if anything else goes wrong because of your stupidity?"

Zhang Qilin turned toward her, the expression in his eyes cold and hard. "Let go of me."

Wen-Jin looked at him, her beautiful face pleading and sad and almost irresistible. As she gazed, Zhang Qilin suddenly glared at her so fiercely that his face turned into a devil's mask and she fell back, loosening her grip on his arm.

She steeled herself to look back at the face that had frightened her but now it was calm, belonging to the boy she knew, who nodded in her direction and said softly, "Thank you."

The other boys who had hung back watching all of this suddenly were eager to join in Zhang Qilin's rebellion, reluctant for him to have the sole glory of discovery. They surged forward in one united crowd, and Wen-Jin knew that without a gun in her hand there was no way to stop them.

Uncle Three had a bad temper and if she woke him up to help her, he would almost certainly begin a fistfight with Zhang Qilin and the whole expedition would fall apart. It would be best, she decided, to take them into the main chamber herself and bring them back as rapidly as possible. She was an experienced grave robber and if this was a normal tomb, she would have no problems leading the group in and then back out.

As Poker-face—or Zhang Qilin as I now thought of him—told Fats and me this story twenty years after it occurred, he skipped rapidly over the trip to the tomb, because it was the same as our own—the traps, the staircase in the pool. And, like us, by the time he and the others reached the tablet at the bottom of the pool, they were shaken and apprehensive.

The only one whose eyes held no fear was Zhang Qilin and when Huo Ling noticed this, her infatuation with him grew stronger than ever. "You cowards," she taunted the others in her group. "You're all older than Zhang Qilin but he has more courage than all of you put together. He's the only real man in the bunch."

Eager to regain Huo Ling's good opinion, the others all rushed to get ahead of Zhang Qilin, straight into the center of the mist that lay before them. In a minute, the boy at the head of the pack turned and raced back up the stairs. "There's a monster down there," he shouted as he ran.

Terrified, they all began to retreat, except for Zhang Qilin. Followed by a few of his companions, he walked into the mist to face the monster, which turned out to be nothing more than the monkey statues.

And then they found the tablet.

"Incredible," Wen-Jin exclaimed. "This place is beyond imagination. It could become another of China's archaeological milestones."

The group of students began to think of the fame that would be theirs and burst into wild chatter, all fear forgotten, but Zhang Qilin stared at the tablet and realized as he looked that words began to form on its surface: "The doorway to the Palace of Heaven shall appear to those whose destiny is tied to this tablet. Once entered, paradise will be reached."

His mind was pierced by these words and he could think of nothing else. Why was he the only one who could see these words and what did they mean? Where was the doorway, and what did it mean to have a "destiny tied to this tablet"? He stood in front of the words and searched carefully. There was no entryway anywhere to be seen, nor did any other words come into his view. He was baffled.

Meanwhile Wen-Jin began to gather her group together for their return to the ear chamber where Uncle Three still slumbered. One by one, she counted the students and discovered that Zhang Qilin wasn't there.

Damn that boy, she fumed silently, first he insists on coming to this place and now he refuses to leave—I should just leave him behind. But her sense of responsibility was too strong; she gathered the others together and led them back into the mist.

After a few steps, they saw Zhang Qilin squatting in front of the plaque, deep in concentration. Wen-Jin's temper flared and she screamed, "Why are you still here? How much more difficult will you insist on making my job..."

Before she could finish speaking, she was interrupted by someone grabbing her hand and stuttering, "No! Don't say anything more." It was Huo Ling, pointing into the mist and looking frightened. Wen-Jin stared off to the spot where the girl's hand was outstretched and saw a large human shadow standing not two feet away from Zhang Qilin.

CHAPTER THIRTY-TWO

STRANGE DOOR AND FLYING ARMOR

The enormous silhouette was nearly the same height as the stone tablet; it had a head and a neck and looked not that different from a man, except it was hunched over from the waist up. It looked abnormal and rather hideous and as she looked at the giant shadow, Wen-Jin had to force herself to keep breathing. Whatever it was, it stood only about five paces away from her and the group of students.

And this damn Zhang Qilin had no idea this creature was here; he was frozen in place, only aware of the tablet before him. Huo Ling broke the silence, whispering, "Young Zhang, why are you still squatting down there? Come with us quickly!"

Wen-Jin put her hand over the girl's mouth and thought desperately of what could be done. She didn't think the giant was a zombie; the Feng Shui of this tomb was too good for them to have taken hold here. It had to be an animal or a human being, and with as many people as were in her group, they could overpower any living being without too much difficulty. Even if it was a giant.

"Look Wen-Jin, this thing is standing exactly where the monkey statues are," one of the boys whispered.

"Could there be something standing on top of one of the monkeys?"

Damn it, Wen-Jin thought, it's that stupid man of mine, Wu Sansheng. He probably woke up, found we were missing, and came to teach us all a lesson. Intolerable!

Certain she was correct, she called toward the giant, "Wu Sansheng! Stop fooling around! Come down right now!"

As her voice trailed away, the shadow suddenly stretched out an arm and waved at her as if to say shut up, and Wen-Jin saw clearly that the shadow was completely out of proportion. It was certainly somebody standing on the statue and it had to be their captain, Wu Sansheng. In a fury, she rushed toward him. It was definitely time to stop this idiocy.

As she reached the form on the statue, it grabbed her and held her tightly in its arms. Covering her mouth, the figure whispered, "It's Young Zhang. Don't talk! Just look down!"

Wen-Jin was boiling with rage but when she heard the voice, she turned to ice. It really was Zhang Qilin's voice, but how could he be standing on the monkey statue?

Her thoughts veered wildly into another direction, and she shivered. If Zhang Qilin held her now, then who was standing in front of the tablet? She looked down at the figure—it was a man wearing a wet suit—it was indeed their leader, Wu Sansheng.

And there was something wrong with him. He stood before the tablet as though it were a full-length mirror, carefully combing his hair as though he were a woman. When he was satisfied with the way his hair looked, he looked carefully at his face in the surface of the tablet, as though he was a young girl examining her makeup. It should have been comical but as Wen-Jin watched, she felt terror seeping across her body and into her heart and lungs.

The students saw Wen-Jin in the arms of the shadow and thought it had to be Wu Sansheng holding her. Relieved, Huo Ling ran to the figure she thought was Zhang Qilin and patted him on the shoulder. "Wake up, Young Zhang," she laughed.

Atop the statue, Zhang Qilin muttered, "That stupid little bitch," but he could do nothing to stop what was happening below. The man in front of the tablet leaped to his feet and Huo Ling screamed. When she saw who it was, her fear quickly turned to petulance and she scolded, "For heaven's sake, Wu Sansheng, what are you doing here, squatting like a crazy person? We all thought you were asleep."

Uncle Three saw Huo Ling, covered his face, screamed, pushed her to the floor, turned, and ran off into the darkness. Zhang Qilin immediately jumped down from the monkey statue and chased after him. He was remarkably swift, but when he passed Huo Ling he stopped to see if she was hurt. And it was precisely this polite and caring gesture that kept him from success— when Huo Ling saw that Zhang Qilin had come to check on her safety, she was sure that he cared about her and she clutched him in a firm embrace.

Damn this girl, Zhang Qilin thought, a few seconds of delay is all that Wu Sansheng needs to get away. He tore himself from the hug in time to see his quarry race into the fog, already almost at the staircase.

"Run for the stairs, all of you! Don't let him go up!" He called to the others as he ran. He saw the shadow of Wu Sansheng turn. It seemed to melt into the wall, but the thick fog kept him from seeing clearly if this really had happened.

When he reached the edge of the pool, there was nobody in sight. Impossible that he could slip into the wall, Zhang Qilin muttered to himself. Where is that damn idiot? There's some trick going on here.

He stretched out his hand to feel the wall; the bricks were solid and he was sure no human could pass through them. He extended his two freakishly long fingers and touched the bricks again. This time his sensitive fingertips could detect motion; the bricks in the wall were moving very, very slowly. Shit, he thought, we're all done for. This entire pool is one enormous trap, a miracle of ancient engineering skill.

But what is the purpose of this trap? Why is it here?

Zhang Qilin had studied the art of ancient traps and he would tell anyone without any false modesty that he knew and understood more about the traps in ancient tombs than anyone else in the world. He knew everything about every trap, its method, its flaws, its origin, and even the name of the man who invented it. And he knew that the trap he had just encountered used the simplest of principles that would not erode over time—stone and running water which would change direction with the changing tide. This is why it was still effective after thousands of years. It had to have been invented by Wang Canghai.

As Zhang Qilin reflected on the skill of the man whose mind and soul were inseparable, his hands kept exploring the wall before him. There had to be a door through which Wu Sansheng had escaped, a door that had moved slowly away with the motion of the bricks in the wall. And suddenly there it was—a trapdoor.

Too easy, he told himself, keep looking. Sure enough, he counted eight trapdoors, lined up in a very small space. Impossible, he thought, could this possibly be the embodiment of Strange Door and Flying Armor?

32. STRANGE DOOR AND FLYING ARMOR

CHAPTER THIRTY-THREE
THE LIVING DOOR

Strange Door and Flying Armor is a complex and arcane discipline that is almost as old as the history of China. It came from the legendary master, Ancestor Huandi, over forty-six hundred years ago and has influenced the art of warfare ever since. Over the years it has been summarized and simplified and few people understand it now, except that it was originally devised for efficiency on the battlefield.

It is also known as the Eight Doors: the Opened Door, the Unused Door, the Living Door, the Death Door, the Fear Door, the Injury Door, the Closed Door, and the Landscape Door. One would live after going through the Living Door, and die after going through the Death Door. Entering any other door would lead one back to the eight doors, and the cycle would begin again.

When Zhang Qilin came upon the eight trapdoors, Strange Door and Flying Armor immediately sprang to his mind. Did these doors hold the same fates for those who entered them, he wondered? And which one did Wu Sansheng choose? All of the doors were quite narrow; to enter one of them, even a very slender person would have to turn sideways.

He went back to the group and told them what he had found. Few of them knew what he was talking about, since many of the ancient disciplines had been suppressed during the Cultural Revolution, but Wen-Jin knew. Looking troubled, she said, "Wu Sansheng's behavior a moment ago was really strange, as if he was possessed by the ghost of a woman. Could that spirit be the owner of this tomb? And the trapdoor he just entered—could that be the Living Door?"

Zhang Qilin saw a spark in her eyes as if she had just thought of something, and asked, "Something comes to mind?"

They all followed Wen-Jin as she walked to the tablet. Copying what she had seen Wu Sansheng do, she began to comb her hair exactly as he had done, then slowly turned her head from left to right. Jumping to her feet, she cried, "I found it!"

The students crowded around her, looking at the tablet but they saw nothing.

"No, not like that!" Wen-Jin remonstrated. "That's not right. You have to do what I did while kneeling in this spot if you want to see it."

Zhang Qilin knelt down and Wen-Jin pressed his shoulders, saying, "You're too tall. Bend a bit lower. And don't look straight ahead. Try to see the temples of your forehead and then peek out from the corner of your eyes."

Feeling a bit silly, Zhang Qilin copied what he had seen Wu Sansheng and Wen-Jin do, first combing his hair and then glancing sideways like a demure young girl. Suddenly he saw himself reflected in the surface of the tablet, but where his temples should have been were three small and shadowy fish, all linked together. He moved his head very slowly and the image instantly disappeared.

So that is the destiny that is linked to the tablet, he realized. Only a vain and lovely woman who was just the right height and who spent time gazing at her own reflection would ever be able to see the three fish in the tablet. If it hadn't been for Wen-Jin's feminine outlook and her keen powers of observation, neither he nor any other man would ever have figured it out—except of course for Wu Sansheng. How did he ever know this secret?

He stealthily peered at the fish, and saw that, like the pool's brick walls, this image was also slowly moving. On the other side of the fish must be the Doorway to Heaven.

He motioned for Wen-Jin to continue staring at the image while he ran to the side of the pool and beamed the ray of his flashlight on each trapdoor one by one. When he illuminated the third door, Wen-Jin saw that the imprint of the fish was caught in the flashlight's beam and she shouted, "This is the door!"

Zhang Qilin raised his fist in triumph as his companions all cheered. Forcing open the trapdoor, he slid through the narrow opening and carefully began to explore the sloping passageway within. He felt about for traps and, finding none, called the rest of the group to follow him.

Leading the way, Zhang Qilin aimed his flashlight into the darkness and saw the walkway was made of blue bricks that looked like a hallway for the dead under the dim light. He moved ahead silently and the others followed his example, making no sound as they cautiously advanced.

33. THE LIVING DOOR

They walked on for the amount of time that it would take to smoke half a cigarette, feeling as though they were the only living creatures left in the entire universe. The passageway took an upward turn and in the distance a light shone, dim and pale like a fading sunset.

Zhang Qilin could feel warmth radiating from the shaft of light and knew they were at the end of the hall. He yelled, "Come on," and rushed ahead of the others. He stopped abruptly with a shout and wavered as though he was going to fall on his knees. "What the hell," he shouted, "the whole world is awash with golden light. What is this?"

His companions ran to his side and saw before them a huge rectangular room that looked completely majestic. It was easy to understand why Zhang Qilin had almost knelt when he first saw it.

On each side of the room were ten golden columns made of nanmu wood, so large that they couldn't have been encircled by the joined arms of three men, looking like the columns that stand in the four corners of the world to support heaven. The walls were at least a hundred feet long and the ceiling beams were ornately carved with ten magnificent golden five-clawed dragons. A map of fifty stars was inlaid on the ceiling, each star a gleaming pearl the size of a goose's egg, and each bathed in a soft yellow light. Their glow was caught in huge mirrors placed in each corner of the room and that reflection was enough to illuminate the cavernous chamber.

In the center of the room was a mammoth stone tray that held what Zhang Qilin realized was a gigantic model of a palace that looked familiar. He ran over to examine it. It looked exactly like the Palace of Heaven that he had seen painted on the small double-handled pot.

Was it possible? Were they now above the clouds, floating through the sky in this magnificent room?

As the students pushed closer to look at this discovery, they became boisterous with excitement and one boy picked up Huo Ling and put her in the very center of the stone tray. She giggled and then shrieked, "Get me down from here. There's a dead body in the middle of this place!"

Zhang Qilin sprang up into the tray in one leap as the boys removed the hysterical Huo Ling. In the middle of the palace was a circular garden of jade boulders and within that, sitting upright on a pedestal, was a shrunken, mummified corpse. Its tattered clothing revealed a torso that had turned black.

This, Zhang Qilin knew, was a rare, seated Golden Corpse that had been dried naturally by strong gales of wind. One of its hands pointed to the sky and the other toward the ground. Its hair and fingernails had continued to grow after death, and its nails were almost as long as its fingers, giving the body a bizarre appearance. Zhang Qilin shuddered and then jumped up beside the corpse. He opened its mouth, and finding nothing inside it, he stuck his hands under the dead man's armpits and pushed hard.

Suddenly Wen-Jin stood beside him, asking, "Zhang Qilin, who are you and where do you come from? Who taught you to be a grave robber?" He looked at her in silence and her temper rushed back into flame. "Don't deny that's what you are. I can tell from your actions. Why did you come with us?"

33. THE LIVING DOOR

Zhang Qilin put his fingers to his lips, then pointed to the corpse saying, "None of that is important. Look here!" He removed the scraps of clothing from the body, exposing a very long scar on the stomach that stretched all the way from the last rib on the left to the lower part of the abdomen. He pressed upon the mummy's stomach, then took Wen-Jin's hand and pressed it down upon that same spot. Wen-Jin drew back and whispered, "Yes, there's something hidden in there."

Zhang Qilin raised his head, unsure whether to remove the object from the body or not. His code of honor demanded that he never destroy a corpse in an ancient tomb for his personal gain. If this person had swallowed something before he died, it must have been very special to him. Or could this be a test that the dead man had set for those who might find his corpse?

He looked questioningly at Wen-Jin, who was from the northern faction of grave robbers and therefore had high moral principles about her trade. She gave a determined shake of her head and said, "Those who remove objects from within a dead body have no heart and will surely be judged harshly by heaven."

Zhang Qilin sighed, stepped back, and bowed in homage to the corpse. When he stood upright once more, he gasped, "Wen-Jin, look. The corpse has begun to smile."

CHAPTER THIRTY-FOUR
CHAIN

Not only did the corpse have a grim smile on its withered face, the hand that had pointed at the sky had moved as well and was now horizontal, stretching eastward. Then the pearls on the ceiling grew dim, lost their light, and the gigantic chamber was lost in darkness.

Some of the students screamed. Zhang Qilin realized he could still make out their forms in the blackness and saw that one star at the corners of each of the four walls still emitted light, like tiny street lights at midnight. Then he heard one of the group quaver, "Look—on the wall—there's a face."

Turning, Zhang Qilin saw, near the star on the eastern wall, a large and hideous face gleaming in the darkness.

"It's a trick," he yelled to his comrades and leaped from the platform toward the brick wall on the east. "It's only a painted mural—come and see." As he looked closer, he discovered what first appeared to be a threatening visage was actually a landscape painting, showing the same Palace of Heaven that he had seen earlier on the double-handled pot. But in this painting it was obvious that the so-called Palace of Heaven was actually built on a very high mountain that was shrouded in misty clouds. The peak gleamed with snow so he knew its elevation was lofty, but the painting gave no clue as to which mountain it might be.

He looked around and saw paintings on all four walls. The painting on the southern wall showed a long line of workers using a massive hoist to lift a gigantic coffin upward to the top of a steep cliff. A funeral procession was waiting in a line, as those in the lead ascended a boardwalk that snaked along the mountainside. Was this Palace of Heaven a tomb, Zhang Qilin wondered, and who was the person in that coffin?

He walked on and found that the mural on the west wall was even more enigmatic. Fires blazed skyward on the boardwalks, probably set by military guards after the funeral ceremony. In order to ensure the safety of the mausoleum, the one and only pathway to the coffin was destroyed to prevent robbery and desecration. With no path, who would ascend such a steep and lofty cliff no matter what was rumored to be at the top?

Quickly he ran to the last painting, and stood before it in a stupor of amazement. The Palace of Heaven had disappeared. All that could be seen was a dazzling blanket of piercingly white snow that covered every cliff in sight. It was an avalanche, Zhang Qilin thought, how brilliant was that? Nobody would ever know the Palace had ever been there. The heat of the fires had warmed the tons of snow on the mountain and had created the ultimate mausoleum, burying the Palace and the tomb forever. What an ending to such magnificence, he sighed.

How could someone as brilliant as Wang Canghai bear to watch his achievement of a lifetime be obliterated so completely? No wonder he had to record the matter so secretively—he had to find some way to show future generations that this stunning creation was part of his life's output.

But who had been buried in this tomb? Zhang Qilin took a deep breath as he launched on this new line of questioning, but then he saw Wen-Jin and a few of the students trying to move the large mirror in the southeast corner of the room. "What are you doing?" he called and she replied, "I just saw Wu Sansheng hiding behind the mirror. But then, in a flash he disappeared."

He hurried over to help. The mirror was made of bronze and gold and was extremely heavy. With all of them working to push it, they managed to budge it only by a few inches, just enough to reveal a hole in the wall that was about the size of half a man. When they shone their flashlights within the opening, all they could see was darkness. "God only knows where this leads," Wen-Jin said sadly and Zhang Qilin muttered, "Maybe so, but I can find out," as he plunged through the opening.

The others followed as quickly as they could. "Everyone but those in front turn off your flashlights to save battery power," Wen-Jin ordered as she and Zhang Qilin led the way.

"There's something crawling in front of us," Zhang Qilin said to Wen-Jin. "Can you see it?" "No," she answered, "but I smell that same fragrance in the air that filled the room when Wu Sansheng fell asleep so quickly. I'm afraid, Young Zhang. There's something wrong here."

Soft thudding sounds came from behind them and when they turned, they saw several of the students had fallen to the ground. Wen-Jin rubbed her forehead and looked dizzy, and then her knees buckled. Zhang Qilin caught her as she fell, feeling disoriented and wobbly himself. He held his breath against the sweetness in the air but it was too late. His eyes drooped and he leaned back against the wall to keep his balance. The last thing he saw before he lost consciousness was Wu Sansheng crouched before him, staring at Wen-Jin as if she were a stranger.

Qilin's story ended here, as abruptly as my Uncle Three's story did when he told it to me. He resumed in the same way my uncle did. "When I woke up, I was lying in a hospital bed, unable to remember anything. A few months later, bits and pieces of memories returned to me. And now, after so many years, I've discovered a problem has developed in my body."

I wanted to ask him if he found he was unable to grow old, but he kept talking. "I can't tell you what it is now. But three months ago when I bumped into your Uncle Three, I noticed he looked very familiar. In order to recall more of what had happened, I followed you guys to the tomb of the Ruler of Dead Soldiers and," he paused, turned to me, and said, "then I found there was something very wrong with your Uncle Three."

"What the hell do you mean?" I asked and he continued, "The silk manuscript you guys took from the bronze coffin was fake. It had been left by your uncle when he took the real one."

"Bullshit!" I yelled. "You switched the damn thing."

Qilin stared at me as though he felt sorry for me and said, "No. It was your Uncle Three who did it. He and Big Kui, the two of them, they dug from behind the tree and directly into the coffin and switched manuscripts when we were digging on the other side. That's why Big Kui had to die."

The more I listened to him, the sicker I felt. Although I still wanted to defend my uncle, countless scenes flashed before me. I recalled how Big Kui was poisoned, why Panzi was still conscious before he climbed the hydra-cypress but had fallen into a deep coma by the time we saw him above ground, and how Uncle Three was already carrying barrels of gasoline over to the cavern's opening long before Fats and I crawled out to safety.

It was impossible to go on thinking this way; I felt like everything in the world had turned upside down and I didn't know who was telling the truth or who was the liar. Was there anyone I could believe? All I could do was mutter to myself over and over, "That's not right. It can't be that simple. There's no motive. Why would Uncle Three do that?"

Qilin said gently, "If this person really was your Uncle Three, then there was no motive. But—," he paused and sighed.

I still didn't understand what he meant, but somehow I began to believe him. Funny, I thought, up until now I was worried about how many lies my uncle told me, when the issue really is, was there anything at all that he was truthful about? So many changes, and I just couldn't absorb them all. But what difference did any of them make if we didn't successfully get out of this damn tomb? Truth or lies would mean nothing to us if we died here.

I did my best to calm down and almost managed it when I saw Fats squatting clumsily in front of the tablet, holding his fingers as thought they were orchids in the hands of a lovely woman, combing his hair as he wobbled in place.

"Damn you, Fats! What the hell are you doing? Can't you just be still for one second and give us a little peace?" I yelled. He turned and answered in a high-pitched falsetto, "Take pity on a poor girl. I only wanted to fix my hair. It won't kill you, so what are you bitching about anyway?"

"Oh shit," I sighed. "So now you plan to comb your way into the Palace of Heaven, do you?"

In his own voice, Fats snapped, "Of course! How could I miss such a spectacular scene? It was no picnic getting here and now that bitch is gone, so is our payment, I'm sure. No problem, I'll make up for that lack with a couple of those goose-egg pearls. As the saying goes, if you're rich, don't bother grave robbing but if you do rob a grave, don't come back empty-handed!"

"So with all that was said, you only heard about the goose eggs, have you, you dumb shit?"

"Don't badmouth me without knowing the facts, Young Wu! There's another very important reason for me to enter this Palace of Heaven. Do you guys want to know what it is or not?"

CHAPTER THIRTY-FIVE
WORDS WRITTEN IN BLOOD

"Come on, Fats," I said, "who doesn't know what you have on your greedy little mind? Don't forget that we're still in trouble so don't start blathering about all your far-fetched mumbo jumbo."

"Don't worry. What I am about to say now is significantly related to the situation we are in. Didn't you listen to that story just now? The corridor to the doorway of the Palace of Heaven goes uphill. And the big room where the model is placed is also located up on a higher plane than we are in now. It's probably at least twenty feet high. Think about how deep this ancient tomb is. I am guessing that the ceiling of that room is the pinnacle of the tomb. We should use our brains to get there if we want to get out of this place to safety."

My mind lit up and I calculated the distance in my head. To my great surprise, Fats was probably right. While I was entranced in the story, he was putting together all the details. He looked like a pig, but his brain worked just fine. "You have a point, Fats," I conceded, "but it does us no good when you think about it. We have no weapons or tools in our hands so how do we make our way through layers of bricks at the top of the tomb? I say we first find a few sturdy metal funeral objects and carry on with our original plan of digging a tunnel to get out. If we don't hurry, we're going to miss the high tide."

As I said that, I realized the only objects we had found were made of porcelain or stone, and no metal of any kind, which was so unusual that I knew it was deliberately planned by the tomb's occupant. If we didn't find something useful soon, we would certainly die here.

Fats laughed belittlingly and said, "Yeah, I already thought of that. Aren't there four bronze mirrors in that room? You're in the antique business. You know what these mirrors look like, right? We'll take off the legs of the mirror—they'll be heavy as sledgehammers."

What he just said sounded very familiar, and I knew I'd done something like that before but I couldn't remember where or why. "Okay," I told him, "let's do it. But when we reach this place, you can't touch anything, promise me. There will be traps everywhere. We still have a lot of life left to enjoy and it's not worth it to stay here forever just for a few pieces of a dead guy's stuff."

Fats nodded. "I won't touch anything but the mirrors and the bricks," he promised.

"Don't even look at those fucking pearls," I warned him, and he rolled his eyes. "Didn't I promise? Drop it."

We went over our plan several times, then found the doorway to the Palace of Heaven and made our way down the narrow corridor.

Qilin had described this place to us but that didn't prepare me for the claustrophobic panic I felt after a few minutes in total darkness and—what was even worse—silence. All I could hear was the patter of our rubber slippers, which sounded as though a monster was tailing us. I tried not to think about the sea monkey.

Fats was annoyed that his bulk could barely squeeze down the hallway and kept up a long string of curses as he walked. Suddenly he yelped, "God damn it, I'm stuck. Help me!"

I had to force myself to stop laughing. As I touched the sides of the passageway, I realized it had become narrower. "Fats, the farther we go, the narrower this becomes. Take a step back and see if you can move."

Shaking his butt, Fats did his best to step backward with no success. "You're wrong. Now the tunnel behind us is narrower than it was a minute or two ago. What's going on here?"

I put one hand on each side of the corridor and felt something peculiar. "Shit," I yelled, "these walls are pressing inward toward each other!"

Qilin shouted, "You're right, I feel it too. Go back fast!"

This trap was going to turn us into three pancakes, it was obvious. I turned and ran and Fats squeezed free with a burst of strength, yelling, "Wait for me, you selfish bastards."

I ran faster than I ever had before and even so, by the time I reached the doorway that had led us to this damn corridor, the walls had almost come together and Fats was walking sideways like a giant crab. Qilin pulled at the doorknob, turned it twice, and shouted, "Someone has locked the door on the other side!"

Fats yowled, "Damn it all, we're done for. Think of something fast or we'll be dead in a minute."

I said, "What solution is there? Just run to the door to the Palace. Perhaps we'll still have a chance to live if we are fast enough!"

Qilin pulled me back, shook his head, and said, "It will take at least ten minutes to get to the other side and that will be too late. Let's climb up and take a look!" Then he leaped along the sides of the walls and began to climb. I looked up. It was just as dark above as it was where I was standing. I could see no change in the width, and did not know whether Qilin's plan would work. But it was better than waiting here to die. I quickly called over to Fats, "Start climbing or plan to get a lot thinner soon."

Because the corridor was so narrow, climbing was as easy as walking. We kept going, and in a few minutes we had climbed up about twenty feet. "Thank goodness this guy is so quick-witted," Fats observed. "This is great. We can jump and commit suicide before we're smashed into pancakes! That way, there'll be no pain at all!"

I couldn't tell whether he was being sarcastic or not, but I was ready to puke when I thought of being pressed into a hamburger patty—not the way I wanted to die. I might even hear the sound of my own skull being crushed. I really would rather die from a fall than be smashed to death, I decided, and then Qilin shouted from above, "Stop imagining things. We still have time. Do you guys remember the robbers' tunnel under the coffin?"

"Of course I remember," Fats grumbled. "But what does that have to do with us now?" His voice had hardly faded before he added, "Oh, I get it. You're saying that we should learn from the robbers and never give up until the last minute, right?"

35. WORDS WRITTEN IN BLOOD

"No, there isn't a grave robber in the world who would dig a tunnel in a grave to get around if there are paths for him to walk on. With these corridors, there's only one reason for a tunnel, he dug it so he could escape."

"You mean that the person who dug the tunnel was in the same situation as we are now, and that he had to dig his way out?" I asked with a quick flare of hope. Suddenly I understood why Qilin had told us to climb. The corridors were made of white jade and we couldn't get through them without dynamite. The only place for us to dig would be the ceiling.

"Hell," Fats said, "this is a long fucking corridor. What are we going to do if the tunnel's entrance is on the other end?"

"Anyone facing this situation would certainly run for the exit first," Qilin explained. "Only if he found the door at the exit was jammed would he turn to the last resort of digging a tunnel. Therefore, the opening should undoubtedly be in this vicinity. If he did dig it on the other side, then we're dead men."

His point was convincing and Fats and I joined him in searching along the sides of both walls. Fats, however, had a problem—he could only move by pulling in his belly, which was quite an energy drain. I tried to console him by saying that fat was easily compressed and he was sure to make it with no problem as long as his weight didn't cave in his bones. He looked as though he'd enjoy caving in my bones but fortunately was in no position to do anything.

We climbed along the walls for quite a while but found nothing. It was more exhausting to climb sideways than it was making the ascent, and my legs began to shake.

I began to think about the sea monkey and realized I'd rather be eaten by him than be squashed between two walls. Even the corpse-eating bugs from our last adventure began to seem almost endearing compared to the death we faced now.

"Come here," Qilin called, and Fats and I both knew he had found the tunnel's opening. Quickly we squeezed our way to his side and saw above our heads on the ceiling a long row of words written in blood. "Wu Sansheng harmed me. I came to a dead end, and suffered an unjust death. Heaven and Earth will punish him for what he has done to me—Jie Lianhuan."

"This…," I stuttered, "what does this mean? Who is this? Why did he say Uncle Three hurt him?"

"Jie Lianhuan was one of the people on the archaeological excavation team. He was the one who died in the reefs clutching the Bronze Fish with Snake Brows."

"What?" I was confused all over again. Qilin gave me a push and said, "He left his words here, yet he wasn't crushed here. It shows that the robbers' tunnel must be nearby. We don't have time to think about what this means. Let's keep moving."

Jie Lianhuan, I thought as I climbed. Why did this name sound so familiar?

CHAPTER THIRTY-SIX

SAVED FROM THE TUNNEL

It was no wonder I couldn't remember who Jie Lianhuan was. As the saying goes, cousins are always three thousand miles apart, and this guy had been a cousin's cousin, born into a family who had been grave robbers for generations. Jie Lianhuan was a prodigal son who had a lot in common with my Uncle Three, so the two of them became very close friends and colleagues.

When my grandfather berated Uncle Three, he would frequently mention the Jie family, yelling that we would never be able to hold up our heads before them because their son met his death while under my uncle's leadership. Jie Lianhuan was a name that everyone in my family did their best to forget; Uncle Three never talked about him at all.

Now it was obvious that Jie Lianhuan had died on this undersea expedition, and quite possibly because of my uncle. No wonder my old man would not let me go on grave-robbing adventures with his brother—the guy had a previous record as a menace to society.

Fats had caught up with me, grunting curses at my slowness, so I stopped fitting puzzle pieces together in my mind. As I moved ahead a step or two, I was sure I saw a dark opening on the ceiling of the rapidly narrowing corridor but couldn't quite believe my eyes until I heard Fats say happily, "Look at that will you? Just when I was ready to die…" I looked back at him and saw he truly had reached his limit. His bulging body was rubbed raw, as red as if he had just been parboiled in a Turkish bath.

Qilin disappeared into the hole in the ceiling and I could hear him kicking the walls of the tunnel within to test their strength. He reached out and pulled me up through the opening and then we both wrestled to bring Fats to safety. Once we were all inside the tunnel, we looked back down to where we had been moments before and Fats muttered, "Fuck me, aren't we the lucky ones?" The walls of the corridor were now separated by a thin sliver of space; not even Qilin's narrow body would have fit in that little slit.

We then examined our place of refuge. It was a robbers' tunnel, with just enough space for us to stand upright and walk in single file. It led upward in a vertical ascent, then changed angles and went horizontally to the east. We climbed as quickly as we could to the horizontal path and then collapsed, gasping for breath. As we panted, we heard the stone walls below us slam together. There was no other way out now but the path before us.

Exhausted by our escape, we all sat as still as corpses. Fats yawned and said, "I swear to every ancestor I have ever had that when I get out of here, I will lose fifty pounds in a week. Look at me—I've already lost five pounds just scraping my skin along that murderous corridor that just tried to kill us."

36. SAVED FROM THE TUNNEL

I cast the beam of my flashlight into the tunnel and saw it had been dug in the shape of the letter S, which meant that even if a portion of it collapsed, there was a chance that we would not be buried in rubble. If Jie Lianhuan had dug this, he wasn't a complete fuckup after all.

Fats had finally recovered his breath and his love of his own voice returned to him. "Someone tell me, why did a path that was walkable twenty years ago suddenly become a route that almost crushed us to death? Did we take a wrong turn somehow?"

Qilin closed his eyes meditatively, was silent for a minute, and then answered, "No, I think someone switched the image that marked the Living Door so we entered the Death Door instead."

"But who?" Fats asked. "Could Ning have followed us and tried to kill us?"

I shook my head. "She's a real bitch but I don't think she had the skill or the knowledge to pull off that trick." Then I stopped talking as the thought occurred to me that the person who tried to kill us might have been my Uncle Three.

Qilin saw my expression become troubled and patted my shoulder. "I have a theory," he told us. "See if you agree with it." Fats and I both looked at him expectantly.

Let's assume," he began, "that twenty years ago your uncle and Jie Lianhuan were friends but joined this expedition pretending that they didn't know each other. When our group went down on their first dive, Jie Lianhuan probably found the undersea tomb then and told nobody but his good friend Wu Sansheng. Grave robbers that they were, they were determined not to let this opportunity slip past them. Together they returned when the rest of the group was preoccupied and entered the tomb. Somehow Jie Lianhuan realized your uncle intended to kill him and left behind his bloody message. As he wrote, he discovered the bricks on the wall were hollow ones and dug this tunnel to escape from his murderer. He found his way out of the tomb, but your uncle found him, killed him, and left his body trapped in a coral reef."

I felt sick but had to admit this all made sense and continued to listen without argument. "Because we needed to escape the storm," Qilin went on, "Wu Sansheng led us all into the undersea tomb and pretended to fall asleep, but he didn't expect that I would discover the information painted on the porcelain funeral objects or that I would take my companions to the bottom of the pool. He followed us, pretended to be possessed by the ghost of a woman, and then lured us to the gigantic chamber with its tunnel behind the mirror. He drugged us into unconsciousness; who knows what he did after that. But I am sure that others in the group survived, somehow made their way out of the tomb, and like me, lost their memories. Even if we somehow found each other, without memory, we would have no way of knowing that we had ever met before."

"Why didn't my uncle just kill you all? Wouldn't that have been a more efficient way for him to solve his problem?"

"I have no idea," Qilin replied. "Maybe he thought it would be less trouble to take away our memories."

According to his theory, my uncle was a satanic monster, and that was not the man I knew and had loved since childhood. Before I could argue this point, Fats said, "Young Wu, I've just remembered something that could help explain all this, but promise you won't laugh at me."

"Tell me, go ahead, I promise," I begged and he whispered, "It's simple. Your uncle came here and discovered something...unclean, and fell into a trap. Didn't this guy just say Wu Sansheng was combing his hair like a woman? Didn't he show you the way to the doorway of the Palace of Heaven? How would he know that himself unless he had been possessed by the spirit of the tomb's occupant? When you find your uncle at last, douse him with a bucket of dog's blood. That will exorcise the ghost inside him and then he'll go back to normal again."

I didn't laugh because I'd promised, but this was the biggest bunch of bullshit that Fats had ever come up with. "That's absurd," I told him. "My uncle and I have known each other for my entire life and have worked together for the last twenty years—he has never behaved like a woman."

"I didn't say the ghost was that of a woman," Fats argued. "But it could have placed two separate personalities in your uncle's body. Maybe he's a real man when he's with other people and then puts on makeup and embroiders handkerchiefs when he's alone." He raised his sausagelike fingers in a dancer's delicate pose and I thought it was safe to laugh.

"No," Qilin remonstrated, "Fats is actually making sense. That kind of thing happens in tombs like this one."

Encouraged by this unexpected alliance, Fats puffed up importantly and went on. "You see, it's not nonsense—it's all Feng Shui, you have to know Feng Shui. Water moves only until it meets more water. The ghost of this tomb is a water ghost and couldn't leave the water unless it found a host to carry it away. Study Feng Shui, Young Wu, and attain my wisdom."

I almost believed him. "I'll keep that in mind, Fats, and when I find my uncle, I'll ask a monk to bless a Buddha amulet and I'll press it on Uncle Three's forehead. That should rid him of ghosts as effectively as your dog's blood, which frankly makes me want to puke up my guts. And speaking of puking, you are scratching yourself so much that if you don't stop it, I'll be able to see your bones and then I will really throw up."

"I can't help it," Fats replied. "Haven't you two noticed that since we entered this damn tomb, we've been itching like crazy? Or am I the only one?"

36. SAVED FROM THE TUNNEL

CHAPTER THIRTY-SEVEN

FATS AND HIS FEATHERS

Suddenly I remembered my earlier itchiness from sweat getting into the scrapes from the lotus arrows, but that was gone now. I pulled up my shirt and looked at my neck and chest; the swelling had gone away as well as the irritation.

"I did feel that way but not now. It's so humid in here, you may be especially sensitive to the moisture in the air," I told Fats.

"What am I going to do?" he asked, tearing at his skin with his fingernails. "I itch so much I can't move." He rubbed his shoulders against the tunnel wall and left smears of blood as he moved.

"Let me see. Stop your scratching for one damn minute, can't you?" I yelled as I pointed my flashlight at his back. "Fuck you, Fats, you pig! When was the last time you took a bath?"

Sprouting from the wounds on his back were long white feathers. They were one of the most disgusting things I'd ever seen on a human being.

"That's personal," Fats shouted. "I don't have to answer that."

"You don't have to tell me—I know it's been weeks. Fats, you're molding. Your back is covered with white fungus. In another month or two, you'll be a walking coal mine, covered with white coal."

"What are you talking about? How can coal be white? How could I become a coal mine? Will you just give me a straight answer and stop being such an asshole?"

Zhang Qilin came over, with a worried frown puckering his eyebrows. He pressed on Fats's back and black blood oozed from under his fingers. "Stop joking. He's in real trouble. Those arrows were worse than I thought."

"But look," I said, "I was hit by the arrows too. Why don't I have feathers growing on my back?" I remembered suddenly that in the cavern of the blood zombies, the poison that killed Big Kui had no effect upon me or my grandfather before me, and wondered if he had bequeathed me another valuable immunity.

When he heard what I said, Fats began to panic. "What feathers? What are you talking about? Where am I growing feathers?" He began to claw viciously at his back and I grabbed both of his hands. "Don't move," I told him. "You'll end up killing yourself if you go on like that."

"I want to die! Who wants to live with fucking feathers growing from their skin? Give me a knife; I'll cut them out of my body."

When I was small, I had a terrible skin disease that threatened to kill me. My parents found there was only one way to cure it, but it was so disgusting I knew Fats would never agree to let me try it on him.

"I brought some aftershave lotion with me," I lied. "Let me put some on your back and see if it helps at all."

"You fucking city people," Fats groaned. "Who else would bring aftershave to rob a grave? Oh, go ahead. And next time we go on an expedition be sure you bring a deck of cards so we can play a round or two of bridge, okay?"

As he turned his head away, braced for the sting of the lotion on his bleeding skin, I spat two huge mouthfuls of saliva on his back and rubbed it into his wounds. Fats began to scream and cry like a baby. "Damn you, what are you putting on me? Stop it and just cut off my skin like I asked you before."

"Better that you feel pain than that itching, it means this is working. Does it itch now?" I asked him.

Fats stopped writhing and his screams turned to little sighs of relief. "What did you do? It worked! What brand of aftershave was that anyway?"

"Never mind—we don't have time for you to admire my grooming products. Let's get going." And as I said that, for the first time ever, I saw Qilin smile. It came and went so rapidly I thought I'd imagined it. But if he has a sense of humor, I thought, maybe this guy's human after all.

We continued our eastward journey until Qilin announced, "Look—a fork in the path." We directed our flashlights to the left and saw a dead end, sealed off with piles of stone. The right held a steep passage and we silently began to climb up in that direction, all of us tired and moving slowly.

Qilin stopped abruptly and motioned for us to be still. He turned off his flashlight and we followed his example, sitting in absolute darkness without knowing why. We have to trust him, I thought, the son of a bitch is always right.

And then I heard it, the sounds of footsteps overhead. What was above us and who was walking there? My neck began to itch.

Thinking it was from nerves, I touched the back of my neck

and felt something bumpy stuck to my skin. Whatever it was, it felt like warts. I pushed at it, trying to dislodge it. A sweet scent drifted toward my face and there was something squishy under my fingernails.

Revolted, I wiped my fingers on the wall. Was Fats using hair oil now? It must have been on his filthy head for weeks, I thought, and yearned for some bathwater to appear magically in front of me.

My neck itched again and I reached back and threw the wartlike substance against the wall. I reached out and touched it. It felt like hair, a lot of it, tied up in a thick bunch that coiled around my hand like a huge worm. None of us had that much hair; whose was it?

I remembered the deadly mass of hair in the water tunnel earlier and felt my eyes bulge in an attempt to see what was under my fingers. I didn't have the courage to turn on my flashlight. Although my mouth was wide open, I couldn't scream. Then I felt a cold, slender hand touch my cheek and sharp fingernails ran down my neck.

The mass of hair moved and I felt it clinging to my face. As I gathered my strength to leap back, a sweet and lovely voice asked, "Who are you?" and a woman's body moved into my arms. She was small and slender; she put her mouth up to my ear and I could feel her gentle breath on my cheek.

"Please hold me," she whispered and my arms wrapped themselves around her waist. She was naked; her skin was smooth and cold under my hands. Her lips touched my chin. I lowered my mouth in preparation for her kiss when a beam of light struck us from Qilin's flashlight and I was able to see what was in my arms.

CHAPTER THIRTY-EIGHT

MEETING THE FORBIDDEN LADY

Inches away from my eyes was a bloated, pallid face that was almost transparent. Its eyes were completely black with no whites to them at all. It looked like a rotting corpse whose eyes had been ripped from their sockets. I screamed and pushed the creature away from me, crawling forward in a frenzy. Escape was my only thought.

Blocking my way was Qilin, and although he must have seen my terror, he refused to move. I grabbed him by the shoulders and yelled, "Run! There's a water ghost!"

He covered my mouth and said, "Stop screaming. Where? What ghost?"

I turned to point behind me. "There, damn you. Just look!" But there was nothing, no hair, no swollen face, no naked woman. I almost poked Fats in the eye as I pointed and he grabbed my hand.

"Are you crazy, Young Wu?" he scolded me.

In a puzzled frenzy, I looked all about me. Was I hallucinating? Had I gone insane from lack of oxygen? Fats could tell I was in trouble and his voice softened. "Calm down, don't panic. Tell us what you saw."

"It was hair, it was naked, it was a water ghost—and she wanted to kiss me!"

I tried to describe what had happened but my mind could only babble. Fats broke in impatiently, "No, this is impossible. Any ghost would have had to crawl past me to get to you and I felt nothing. You were dreaming—it's normal for young men to dream about naked women. Nothing to be ashamed of there, I used to dream about them every hour when I was your age."

"Don't patronize me, Fats," I yelled. "Feel my neck where the hair touched me. It's still wet."

They both felt the dampness and looked perplexed. "It's from water dripping into the tunnel," Fats said and I replied, "Don't be a fool. Do you see water dripping in here? The place is watertight."

"But there's only one tunnel. Whatever crawled onto you had to go past me," Fats objected.

"You were probably sleeping and didn't feel anything crawling over your fat carcass."

"Fuck you—even if I were asleep I'd feel someone stepping on me. Just look and see if there are any footprints on my back." Fats turned to prove his point and there, clinging to his back, was the creature with the hair.

I stared, unable to speak. Something pulled on my legs and I looked to see hair coiling around my calves. I tried to shake it off but it snaked its way up my body and pushed into my mouth. Then I felt hands yanking on my collar, and Qilin pulled me to his side.

The hair reached for his arms and he stood still. I looked at Fats; he was wrapped in hair as though he was in a cocoon, writhing like a madman. The creature had disappeared and the tunnel was choked with long black tendrils of its hideous hair.

38. MEETING THE FORBIDDEN LADY

Qilin pulled one arm free from the mass that surrounded us and asked me, "Do you have anything you can ignite? This thing is afraid of fire."

I groped in my pocket, found my waterproof lighter, and clicked it into flame. Holding it to the wet hair that coiled around us, I was amazed to see that it burned away our bonds, even though the coils were soaked with water. I rushed to free Fats but as I approached him, the face reappeared from the mound of hair that imprisoned his huge body and headed toward my back.

There was only one thing to do—I lowered my head and butted like a goat. I heard a loud crack and black water gushed from the nose on the ghastly face. My lighter still aflame, I held it up to burn up this monster, but it pulled away from the fire.

So it's possible to frighten a ghost, I thought exultantly. I kicked my leg toward the face, struck it, and watched it retreat into its hair. Then I raised my lighter and waited for it to reappear.

Qilin found a few wet matches in his own pocket and lit them with my lighter. Seeing even more flame than before, the monster shrieked and leaped backward, giving me time to burn away the hair that held Fats prisoner.

The monster was forced back farther and farther by the flame that Qilin brandished before him, until it finally disappeared into the darkness. We looked at Fats and saw that his face had turned blue; his nose and mouth were stuffed full of hair. He was choking to death on it.

I pounded his chest with every bit of strength I had left. He choked, vomited up the hair, and began to breathe. Black liquid gushed from his nostrils, pushing out the remaining hair, and I felt a wild relief. I would have let Fats die before I gave him mouth-to-mouth resuscitation.

"Holy shit," he gasped as soon as he was able to talk, "what the hell was that?"

I flicked off my lighter but I was damned if I was going to let go of it, even though it was red-hot and was burning through the skin on my hand. Qilin had huge blisters on his fingers from holding his bouquet of matches but he didn't seem to be in pain. "I'm almost positive," he told Fats, "that we were attacked by the Forbidden Lady."

I remembered that name from my visit with the antique dealer who tried to sell me his incense burner not too long ago. "What! There really is such a thing? I thought she was only a legend."

He nodded and said, "Many legends are based on fact and I believe this is one of them. They are water creatures, born and raised in that element and they are terrified of fire. Who knows why? It's like zombies and the hooves of black donkeys. We know about fear but we have no idea what causes it. What is clear is that the creature that just attacked us has a brain and is probably nearby somewhere thinking of how to kill us. We have to be careful."

"So weird," Fats marveled. "This tomb has such good Feng Shui. How can there be so many monstrous things inside it?"

I knew nothing about Feng Shui but I had read about the legend of the Forbidden Lady. She was supposed to be the most evil of all ghosts and if she was caught, her arms and legs had to be cut off and then she was buried alive. She was supposed to be attracted by pregnant women for some reason; I thought of the drawings of big-bellied women that I had seen when we first entered this place and felt sure that what we had battled with just now was the Forbidden Lady.

Qilin signaled for us to keep on going along the tunnel; I looked at Fats and he nodded. I clutched my lighter in a death grip and we set off. To my relief I could no longer hear the footsteps above.

We began to walk up a steep, zigzagging path that I hoped would lead us to the walls of the tomb and then to the seabed and open water. There was only one way for us to go and that was straight ahead, so it came as a surprise when Qilin stopped. "Come on," I said and gave him a gentle push.

"I can't," he answered. "We're at a dead end."

I squeezed past him to see for myself. The path was blocked by gigantic slabs of blue granite.

"Help me," I said, as I began to push at one of the obstructions. They weren't as heavy as they looked and we managed to move one slab far enough to make a little crack that we could peer through.

A small shaft of light shone through the crack and we could see a chamber on the other side of the rocks. As we looked, a noise made us look up. One of the gigantic slabs that had towered over us had disappeared.

CHAPTER THIRTY-NINE
SEA MONKEY SKIRMISH

Looking up to the spot where the slab had been, I expected to see my uncle or perhaps Ning but instead saw a large and very unhappy sea monkey glaring down at us, with a speargun protruding from a bloody shoulder. Hell, I thought, we just can't get rid of this thing—too bad we can't fix him up with the Forbidden Lady. They were made for each other.

Something tugged at my ankle and I looked down from the spot where I had climbed to get a firm grip on the slab we had been moving. Zhang Qilin was pulling at me, urging me to come back into the tunnel. I scrambled down rapidly, followed by a very pissed-off sea monkey.

Zhang Qilin and I raced back toward Fats, but there was no refuge there. He was running up the tunnel to us, yelling, "Run, run! The hag is back!" I stared past him and saw a huge mass of hair pouring into the S-curve of the tunnel. Lucky us, I thought grimly, here's the missing half of the perfect couple.

A stab of pain hit my shoulder and I turned my head to find the sea monkey's fangs had sunk deeply into my flesh. With a jerk of its head, it pulled me up into midair. Seeing the speargun close to me, I kicked at it as hard as

I could and buried it even more deeply into the monkey's wounded shoulder. It opened its mouth in a roar of pain and I fell to the floor of the tunnel, rolled, and tried to get to my feet. The sea monkey rushed toward me, teeth bared, reddened eyes fixed upon my neck. Helplessly, I went into a fetal position, knowing I had no way to escape.

Fats leaped from behind, grabbed the sea monkey's right leg, and tripped it as it lunged for me. Together he and the monkey fell and Fats managed to climb on top of the crazed animal, but only for a second. The monkey swept him to the ground with one swipe of its paw, turned to snarl at him, and then leaped back toward me. This thing knew how to bear a grudge and it obviously hated my guts.

I had no weapon and rolled into a tight ball, hoping to die quickly. Go on, bite my neck, rip my head off, I ordered silently, but I wasn't going to be that fortunate. Towering above me, drooling with rage, the sea monkey raised one huge foot and stamped it down on my stomach. All of my breath left my body and I knew my spinal cord had snapped in two. Vomiting blood, I saw a foot come toward my abdomen again and knew I was going to die an agonizing death. Then I heard a crashing sound. The monkey howled and fell on all fours.

There was Fats, a huge bronze mirror in his hands, standing over the sea monkey like a vengeful god. He was shaking with exertion and I was awestruck that he could carry anything as massive as that mirror. If I live through this, I have to be careful to never let this guy get mad at me, I decided.

Before the sea monkey could rise back up on its hind legs, Fats slammed the bronze mirror on its head, turning its face to a mass of bloody pulp. It rolled away from the attack and leaped up onto a column, roaring in Fats's direction.

A column, I thought through my haze of pain. Where did that come from? Slowly I saw that in this melee we had rolled into a room that was filled with a golden light. It was the room that held the model of the Palace of Heaven. I could see its gigantic stone tray, and the murals that Qilin had described. So that's how Fats found that mirror, I thought slowly and stupidly.

Fats was puffed up by his successful assault, taunting the monkey as he reached down for the bronze mirror, but his adrenaline had ebbed and he was no longer able to lift it. Sensing his weakness, the sea monkey sprang upon him and clawed a layer of skin from his forehead. Fats screamed and bit the monkey on its battered face. It leaped away, looking at Fats warily as it planned its next move.

But it was clearly exhausted and badly injured, shaking its head from side to side like a punch-drunk boxer. As it gathered its senses, it noticed Qilin, alone and undefended in the corner, struggling to seal off the opening to the robbers' tunnel by moving one of the huge pieces of slate, slowly, inch by inch. Roaring with pain and rage, the sea monkey rushed toward him. "Watch out!" I shouted, and Qilin dropped and rolled out of the creature's path.

Quickly he got back to his feet, ran toward one of the columns, and leaped. One leg touching the column, he spun in midair and landed astride the sea monkey's hairy shoulders, almost bringing the creature to its knees. It recovered its balance quickly and began moving wildly to shake its rider from its back. Qilin stuck like a tick on a dog, clasped his legs together tightly with the monkey's head between his knees, and twisted his waist violently. There was a horrible snapping sound and the sea monkey's head fell to the floor, its neck broken in a one-second kill.

Fats and I both stared and I remembered when Qilin had appeared at the burial platform of the Ruler of Dead Soldiers, clutching a zombie's bloody, severed head. So that's how he did it, I thought and shuddered. I was in rough company and needed to mind my manners with these two guys.

Without any delay, Qilin rushed back to seal off the robbers' tunnel, where I could see hair coming up through the opening. I ran to help him push the slab into place while Fats grabbed my lighter and burned the strands that had poked up into the chamber, then joined us in moving the stone to cover the entrance.

We heard the Forbidden Lady pound against the slab to break her way in, but Fats calmly placed his massive butt on the stone covering. He sat there for ten minutes as she battered against his weight on the slab without success.

When she finally gave up, Fats breathed one final "Shit," and immediately fell asleep where he sat. Qilin walked over to the corner where Fats had picked up the bronze mirror. I followed him and saw an opening in the place where the mirror had leaned against the wall. It was half the size of my body and so dark that it was impossible to tell where it might lead us.

39. SEA MONKEY SKIRMISH

CHAPTER FORTY

THE MYSTERIOUS OPENING

This opening was where Zhang Qilin lost his memory and his companions. If I were ever to find out what had become of Wen-Jin and whether my uncle was a killer, I would need to go into this darkness to find the truth.

I carefully examined what I could see. It looked a lot like the tunnels in factories where bricks of charcoal were made, not like something that would be added to a tomb. Of course it might hide burial treasures; my grandfather had noted in his journals that secret chambers were not uncommon but were very well camouflaged. This one was not.

Since a mirror had obscured the opening, it might have been constructed for a Feng Shui purpose, to correct or avert some sort of evil. Keeping this in mind, I went to the other three corners of the room to see if they concealed something similar, and then I saw the four murals.

Three things immediately occurred to me as I looked at them. The mountain in the painting had the distinct look of Mount Changbai. The funeral procession was made up of people dressed in the clothing of the Yuan dynasty, and all of the people in the procession were women. Based upon these observations, I felt sure that it would be possible to find the location of the Palace of Heaven. The only problem I could see was that it had been buried in snow for thousands of years and if one false move was made in the excavation process, a new avalanche could bury it and those who quested for it in another icebound prison.

I returned to the opening in the corner and found Qilin still staring into its depths. "I have to go back in there," he told me as I approached.

"No fucking way," I told him. "That's throwing your life away again. What good will it do any of us if you're struck with amnesia for another twenty years?"

"We're not the same, you and I," he replied. "For you this is an adventure. For me it's a twist in my heart that never goes away. If I don't solve this mystery, I will never be truly alive."

"No," I argued. "It's not just you in this predicament. We have to get out of this place alive. That's our top priority. We don't need any extra complications, don't you understand? It won't be long before we use up all the oxygen in this damn tomb and then we'll all suffocate—what good will your discoveries do then?"

"Are you sure we can make our way out of here?" he asked me, and then I realized I hadn't even looked at the ceiling of the chamber we stood in to assess the probability of our escape.

According to everything I had ever read, the ceilings of Ming dynasty tombs were all described as very strong and sturdy. Their beams consisted of the so-called seven horizontals and eight verticals so I expected this place to be constructed in that manner, like an arched dome, high in the center and lower on the two sides. But as I looked at this ceiling, I saw it had followed the structure of land-based tombs; the ceiling was flat.

40. THE MYSTERIOUS OPENING

It was about twenty feet high with no stepping stones to help us climb to its top. All we could do was use the legs of the mirrors to knock a few dents into the sides of the columns, then climb up, crack the surface of the ceiling, and start working with the bricks. We did not have to be too careful as long as our timing was right. Once the antipressure structure above collapsed, then a hole would appear, seawater would flood into the tomb, and we could swim out.

The timing of this plan was crucial. If we didn't do this during low tide, the entire ceiling would collapse from the force of the seawater gushing in and we'd probably be crushed to death.

Explaining this to Qilin, I stressed that we could probably get out safely but once we did, this tomb would be completely destroyed. However, the objects it contained would still be here; he could come back a few days later with better equipment and find what he might need to solve his mystery.

He nodded and Fats, awake for most of my speech, said, "Since that's the case, what are we waiting for? Let's just get started and take care of the columns now to save time."

I glanced at my watch. There were six hours until low tide; we had a lot of time. Shaking my head, I said, "We just exhausted a lot of our physical strength, and we haven't eaten anything. Our energy is gone and we need to rest. After we get out, we don't know what's going to happen. The boat may have already left and without energy we could drown. If we don't rest, we could die even if we get out of here."

"So we still have to wait, God damn it? Okay then. I'll sleep a bit more," Fats groaned. "Wake me up when you're ready to start work."

I found a spot to sit, leaning against the wall, but my

mind wouldn't turn itself off. It insisted on calculating the outline of our escape route once the seawater began to rush in. The tunnel to the bottom of the pool was now closed off. Although it was not sealed, the water flowing out was sure to be slower than water flowing in. A huge amount of water would certainly first rush into the mysterious tunnel in the wall. Although I did not know where this short tunnel would pass to, it would be very problematic if it was connected to another chamber. A vortex might be formed and we could be sucked back into it.

I paused here, and glanced over at the deepest spot that could be seen in the tunnel, trying to figure out a way to block that opening. Then I realized I could stack pieces of palace model to close it off. Estimating the height and width of the opening, I tried to figure what I would need to cover it. And that was when a weird feeling grabbed me and wouldn't let go.

There was something powerful in the darkness of the doorway that forced me to look in that direction. I tried to turn away but my neck had turned to granite and I couldn't move my eyeballs. I felt a horrible kind of worried anticipation, like a starving man holding a bag of food that he couldn't open, and I knew I had to go through that opening to see what was there.

Without thinking, I ran into the darkest part of the tunnel without even turning on my flashlight, not caring where I was going or what might be in this place with me. Suddenly I felt gusts of wind pushing on my back, a sharp pain hit my left knee, and I sprawled flat on my face.

Blood gushed from my nose, my forehead buzzed with pain, but whatever had compelled me to enter this place had lost its power over me. Staring into the darkness, I knew this was a place where I could easily lose my mind—in fact, I almost had.

Looking up, I saw Fats and Qilin running up to me. Beside me a flashlight lay on the ground and I wondered if one of them had thrown it at my leg to stop me.

The two of them grabbed me by the arms and silently began to drag me out of the tunnel. I tried to stand but my knee wouldn't bear my weight. Fats wrapped both of his arms around me and pulled me with every ounce of his bulk. He had tucked his flashlight under his armpit and it swept over the blackness in a random fashion. It struck something with its careening light and I yelled, "Stop! There's somebody there in front of us!"

I knew I had caught sight of a human form and was sure it was Uncle Three. Fats dropped me and turned his flashlight toward where I pointed. A person's back was running away from us, into the depths of the tunnel.

Qilin yelled, "Come on!" and raced after the figure with Fats close behind. I could barely move but hobbled after them as best as I could. As I drew closer, I could see they had caught up with the runner and pushed the body up against the wall of the cave. Fats held up his flashlight and yelled, "Holy shit, it's Ning."

She was a mess, dirty and stinking. Her wet suit was torn and she had blood all over her face. "What the hell happened to you?" Fats yelled. "You stupid bitch, who did this to you?" But Qilin grabbed him by the arm and said, "Stop it. She isn't all there. You're wasting your time."

CHAPTER FORTY-ONE
THE CORAL TREE

Qilin was right. Ning's face was blank, her eyes were sluggish, she neither struggled nor spoke, as if she didn't even know we were there.

"You're right," Fats admitted. "Usually she'd kick my butt if I talked to her like that."

"Were you rough with her when you caught her?" I asked him. "Is that why she's acting as though she's dead?"

"Would I treat a lady like that?" Fats yelled. "Let's hear a little less bullshit from you, Young Wu. If you don't believe me, ask Qilin. He was right there when I pushed her against the wall."

"Shut up, both of you," Qilin said. "She's okay, just in shock. Something's frightened her." He waved his hand before Ning's eyes, snapping his fingers, but she didn't even blink in response.

"What could have frightened her?" Fats shook his head.

"She has no fear, we know that," I agreed. "Don't be fooled, she's faking this."

"That's right," Fats said eagerly. "Let's slap her face and see if she comes around. One or two slaps ought to pull her right out of whatever game she's playing—here, don't worry, I'll take care of this little bitch."

"Damn it Fats, cut it out," I yelled. "You watch too many gangster movies. Who do you think you are anyway, Chow Yun Fat? Look at the shape she's in—all you can think of is hitting her?"

Fats raised his hand, tapped Ning's face a few times, and then looked remorseful. "You're right. I can't hit her. What the hell should we do with her?"

I had no idea whether Ning was faking or if she was really in shock. "We can't do anything right now—let's just tie her up and take her with us. We can hand her over to the police when we get back on land."

"Now you're the one who's nuts," Fats told me. "Are you really that stupid? We're grave robbers, remember? We're going to the police? I don't think so."

I really had gone crazy; after all, I was no longer a law-abiding owner of an antique book business. Quickly I reassured Fats, "I forgot I was no longer a model citizen who can call the police when things go wrong. Forget what I just said—pretend I farted and ignore me."

"Will you two cut it out?" Qilin was examining Ning's vision with his flashlight. "Look, her pupils are dilated. Her reactions are sluggish. This is serious; she's not pretending."

"Do you know what's wrong?" I asked and he replied, "No idea—she needs expert medical care."

I thought of how high-spirited and lovely Ning had been when I first met her a week or so ago and felt sad. Fats shuddered. "This is a dreadful place. Let's take a quick look around to see if there's anything important and then get the hell out of here."

I wanted to leave right now but was embarrassed to say

so, since I was the reason we were here in the first place. I nodded and Fats pointed his flashlight into the darkest part of the tunnel. I could see we were only a dozen steps or so from the end of it but I couldn't see anything more. Fats frowned as though he could and breathed, "You guys, is that a tree?"

I looked harder and could vaguely see a shape with branches, but how could there be a tree growing in an undersea tomb?

"No light, nobody to water it—it can't be a tree," I muttered.

Fats insisted, "It has to be. Look, it's glowing in a weird way. It looks like gold—let's go take a closer look."

"Damn it Fats, I know what you want. Even if it's solid gold, how the hell would we ever take it back up with us?"

"Maybe we can break off some of its branches. Come on, if there was any danger here, we would already have encountered it—don't be such a coward."

Before I could argue any more, Qilin whispered, "Quiet, follow me and don't dawdle." He disappeared into the cave and Fats scooped Ning up, slung her over his back, and followed. I limped along behind him.

Qilin set a fast pace and soon we were at the end of the tunnel. He raised his flashlight and we saw what Fats had discovered.

It was a huge piece of white coral, carved into the shape of a tree with twelve branches and placed in a large pot. From its branches hung many small bells of a golden color, which gave off the glow that had lured Fats. But verdigris seeped from cracks in the golden covering; these bells were probably valueless brass covered with gold plate.

Fats wasn't ready to lose all hope. "Maybe this coral is worth something. What do you think, Young Wu?"

"Not even a little bit," I told him, happy to get back at him for his rudeness of a moment ago, and Qilin nodded in agreement with my assessment.

"Fuck. I thought I was going to be rich."

I laughed and said, "Fats, cheer up. Even if the coral isn't worth much, the bells hanging on it are good."

"I see your dirty smile. Are you blowing hot air again? I've seen many of these broken bells before. They're only about a thousand a piece. What kind of value are you talking about?"

I replied, "It's because of your business mind that you can't see it. To tell you the truth, I can't guess the specific value, but it's definitely worth more than gold of equal weight. You see the patterns on these bells? They date back even further than the Ming dynasty. At that time they were already regarded as antiques. Do you get what I mean?"

Fats thought for a while and still didn't believe me. He was about to pluck one of the bells to have a look when Qilin grabbed him and said, "Don't move."

"What's wrong?"

Qilin ignored him, turned to me, and asked, "Do you remember where you've seen these bells before?"

CHAPTER FORTY-TWO
DILEMMA

A month or so earlier we had entered the cavern of the blood zombies and found attached to the tail of a large corpse-eating bug a bell that looked like these. Inside it was something that resembled a centipede, which made the bell ring as it walked along. The noise sounded like people whispering powerful and evil secrets to each other, which put us all under a spell as we listened. It was only because of Qilin that we weren't still in the cave, transfixed. Uncle Three said later that the bell dated from before the Warring States Period but that he had no precise idea of when it had been made.

I was unsure that these were exactly like the one we had seen before, but if they were and Fats touched one of them, we would be lost. If the sound of the bell in the cave had almost driven us mad, the ringing of forty of them in unison would probably set us at each other's throats.

"How could this tunnel have the same objects that we found in the blood zombies' cave?" Qilin asked. "Could Wang Canghai have been there as well?"

"Maybe he was a grave robber too," Fats blurted out, and Qilin and I both stared at him.

"You could be onto something," Qilin agreed. "Nobody knows what that man did in his early life except that he became well versed in Feng Shui. It would have been an easy matter for him to rob graves. But he came from a prominent family who never had to worry about money, and they would have been disgraced had he gone into the tombs."

"I don't think it's possible," I objected. "If he had been a grave robber, he would have left warnings to his colleagues who would follow him so they would avoid danger. Do you see any signs of that sort here?"

"I've looked, but found nothing," Qilin admitted, and I knew if he didn't see anything, there was nothing there.

I said, "So how do we explain these bells? Could he have been an antique collector and wanted his beloved collection to be buried with him?"

"We've seen no other antiques in this place so I don't think that's a plausible theory," Fats said, then brightened. "Actually, what other people are fascinated by ancient tombs and seek those places?"

"Do you mean that when he was working on the construction of the Palace of Heaven, he dug these up from the building site?"

"Well done, Young Wu. He was the most prominent builder of his time and was sure to have excavated treasures as he worked. When we get back to the real world, it will be easy to find out the areas he worked in and what he might have found in them."

Fats had a logical argument and I was impressed. At the same time I was ready to hurt him if I had to, in order to keep him from touching any of these bells. My

42. DILEMMA

guess was they were the cause of Ning's mental disorder. If she had so much as tapped against the coral tree, it would have set off the ringing of forty clappers, all making a hypnotic and horrible sound. I knew she was sensitive and highly strung and such a noise could have tipped her into insanity. In fact, these bells might have caused Qilin's loss of memory.

As I examined the branches I noticed that the bells were attached to them with copper wires.

Coral is hollow and would echo with any nearby sound, so the ringing of the bells would become amplified as though there were thousands of them instead of only forty. But this was all speculation and I wasn't prepared to voice any of these thoughts, or to test them out either.

"Let's go," Fats urged. "There's nothing here but these damn bells." As we began to walk back through the tunnel, I pondered three questions. When Qilin was lured into this tunnel twenty years ago, what became of the rest of his group? Did my uncle carry them out, and if so how? And what had become of that strong, sweet aroma that Qilin and Uncle Three had talked about when they told me their stories?

The answers lay with my uncle and if we were unable to find him, we would never know the solution to these mysteries.

If Fats was correct and Uncle Three was possessed by the spirit of this tomb, where would he have gone? When he saw Qilin's photograph, why did he say, "I understand now," and what was is it that he understood?

There was a missing chunk in what I had been told and if I were given only one more tiny clue, I would be able to put all the fragments together and link this place with the tomb we found in the cavern of the blood zombies.

We were back in the large chamber with the palace model. Fats put Ning down carefully and said, "Our time is almost up—let's get to work."

Once again I carefully explained our escape route and we started to work toward our goal. Fats was almost maddened by hunger and took that rage out on the columns, trying to beat steps into the nanmu wood, but found the wood was too hard to dent. I began to help him, although his strength far outstripped my own, but together we managed to make foot-sized indentations in the surface of one of the columns.

We cut our wet suits into long strips and tied them into a rope, which we made into a noose and wrapped around the column. Then we began our ascent, so exhausted that every step upward felt like death itself.

"This is wasted energy," Fats panted. "Let me go up and start digging. When the water enters the chamber, you'll float to the ceiling."

"Do you think I'm doing this for the fun of it?" I responded. "You can't do this alone. If there's a layer of sand above this ceiling and you dig into it without thinking, we're all going to die. You need someone with a brain who can assess the situation and then your muscles can take over."

Fats had enough experience to see my point and beckoned for us to follow him.

42. DILEMMA

We gritted our teeth for another half hour before we reached the top and by then Fats was so exhausted that he held onto the column motionless. "Damn it. I'll die before I ever let myself be tortured like this again."

We gave him a long break to catch his breath since we needed his strength when we began to remove the bricks from the ceiling. I tapped on it but Qilin waved my hand away and touched the bricks with his two long fingers. "It's solid," he announced.

Without a word, Fats began to chisel at the cement that covered the bricks, careful not to break our makeshift rope that held us all in place. We grabbed his shoulders, hoping we could stop his fall if he began to plunge, but his sweaty skin was hard to grasp.

The cement came off in large pieces, revealing the blue bricks within. Fats yelled, "Shit. Touch these damn things and tell me if I'm crazy or not." I reached for the bricks, touched one, and began to curse. They were held in place by iron that had been poured into the cracks between each brick.

CHAPTER FORTY-THREE
A BOMB

What the hell were we going to do now? We couldn't move bricks held in place with iron, not even if we had a jackhammer. And we knew there were at least seven layers of them between us and freedom. My plan was bullshit; we were done for.

Fats looked at me and hissed, "Now what, Comrade Architect? Any more brilliant ideas?"

"What else can we do? Keep digging. The bricks are old; perhaps they've weakened over the centuries," I blustered, and Fats fell for the idea.

It was easy for him to crack the bricks but the iron rods were impossible to budge. "No way," he panted. "Chairman Mao couldn't move these with one of his Liberation tanks."

"We're dead," I groaned. "We have only twenty minutes before the tide turns."

Fats blew up. "What the fuck? Don't you remember what Ning said? A typhoon is blowing in and it will probably last a week— seven days, genius boy. If we don't suffocate we'll starve—unless I strangle your worthless bony body and turn you into soup."

"Okay, okay—I blew it. You two are the ones with experience. What's your solution?"

Without a second of hesitation, Fats and Qilin said in unison, "Explosives!"

"Where the hell are we going to find those?" I asked. "We have only twenty minutes left, don't forget."

"Hold on! Stay here and don't move!" Qilin yelled. "I think I know where there might be what we need!" Without waiting for us to respond, he suddenly let the rope go and slid down the column.

Fats glanced at me and I shook my head to tell him I didn't have the slightest clue. I stared down into the chamber below, where Qilin squatted in front of the mummified corpse that lay in the model of the Palace of Heaven. He was groping about, searching for something, and suddenly I realized what he was looking for. He raised the body carefully and Fats grabbed me by the arm and asked, "What's he up to?"

I replied, "This is just a guess, but there could be a trap inside that corpse which is triggered by dynamite. If anyone tried to take the treasures that were hidden inside the body, they would set off the explosives."

"How does he know this?"

"He touched this corpse twenty years ago, so he might have found it out then. You see, he said a moment ago there could be something. That means that he's not sure," I said. "The only thing is we don't know if an explosive that's several centuries old will still work."

By now, Qilin had moved the mummified corpse to the bottom of our column and called up, "Come down and give me a hand."

Fats had already done too much, so I let him sit there and climbed down alone. Qilin put the corpse on my back and tied it tightly with part of the wet suit rope, warning, "Don't bump into anything. If the explosives inside are still good, one slight touch and off it goes."

Seeing the corpse up close, I thought that the description I had been given of it earlier was far from the truth. Its entire body was so black that it gave off an impression of luster as though it weren't made of flesh but of burnished rock. The muscles were all caved in, especially the mouth, which was in the shape of a half smile. It gave me goose bumps and I didn't want it to touch my body at all.

"Are you sure there's nothing wrong with this corpse? I have a feeling he seems to be waiting for some kind of trap to spring upon on us. You see the expression on his face? How come it's so...so..."

"Evil," Qilin finished my sentence. "I don't understand it either. This corpse really makes me uncomfortable too. But he's already mummified, so he can't turn into a zombie."

I nodded. "That's good. Are you sure the explosives inside are still usable?"

"I hope so," he answered, looking grim.

I felt horrible; the corpse's long fingernails hung in front of my face and made me sick. Its unwrapped skin was cold and dry on my bare back; I had never felt dead flesh so close to my own body before but there was no way to get rid of it other than climbing to the ceiling.

Before I took more than a dozen steps, I knew something was wrong. The body against my back felt as though it had expanded in some way. I looked back at Qilin but he seemed to have seen nothing unusual. Fats was urging me on from above and I continued my ascent, reaching the top at last.

Fats looked sick when he got a good look at what I carried, but this was no time for him to be squeamish. "Tie this thing to the side of the column and climb down at once. We'll set off the explosives from the ground. Hurry up, damn it."

As he lifted the body from my back, Fats grimaced. "Why the hell does this corpse have a tail?"

43. A BOMB

CHAPTER FORTY-FOUR
THE WAY OUT

"What tail? Stop fucking with me, Fats," I yelled. "There's no time for your bullshit now."

"Take a look. Are you blind?" Fats pointed, and as I looked I could see something about three inches long sticking out of the base of the dead man's backbone, looking quite a bit like the tail of a cow. Was this the change I had felt as I climbed? Had it just grown in the past couple of minutes?

"Look, Fats, who cares if it has a tail? Just move—move!" I helped him tie the body to the column and tested the tightness of our knots.

We climbed back to solid ground where Qilin had carried Ning to the farthest corner of the chamber. We moved the mirrors in front of us as protective shields. We were all set—now it was time for Qilin to throw a leg broken off from one of the mirrors to hit the stomach of the corpse and detonate the explosives that we hoped it carried.

I looked at my watch—the tide would soon be low and I prayed it would work to our advantage. "Come on," I yelled. "Hit your target!"

As Qilin poised his body into a hurling position, Fats yelled, "Where's the goddamn corpse?"

It was gone.

We rushed under the spot where it had been tied and saw it, crawling on the ceiling behind the column. Its body was cracking and pieces of its blackened flesh were peeling away and falling to the floor. The rope made from our wet suits was still tied about its waist but was stretched to the limit and would soon snap, leaving the body unfettered.

"Hurry up," Fats yelled, "before he gets away! Detonate the explosives now!"

The minute his words were out of his mouth, I felt something rush past my head; a beam of blue light flew directly into the stomach of the corpse.

I screamed. This was happening too quickly; we were all still in the middle of the room, unshielded. As the light flashed, Fats threw himself on top of me, bringing us both to the floor. There was a horrible crash, the whole room shook, and a powerful surge threw us into midair. We spun six or seven times and then fell back to the floor.

My head hit the wall and I lost consciousness. Then my ears buzzed, light struck my closed eyelids, and the sky and earth spun around me. I opened my eyes and saw only yellow dust everywhere. I vomited, then struggled to my feet.

Out of the smoke ran Qilin, yelling, "Are you okay?"

I nodded and the two of us began searching for Fats. He was sitting in a corner, his head bleeding. "Shit," he yelled. "You moved too soon. You could have given us a second to take shelter."

Qilin thrust out his hand; he still held the leg from the mirror. "It wasn't me."

Fats and I stared at him, speechless. Whoever made that throw had extraordinary skills of power and precision. Who could it have been?

All three of us turned to look at the corner of the room

where Ning had been—she was gone.

"That little bitch! She had us all fooled," Fats spat. We looked all over the chamber and found not even her shadow.

Qilin, for the first time since I met him, looked shocked. "This woman really is amazing," I said in an attempt to console his bad judgment. "I don't think anyone could have guessed she was faking."

Fats agreed. "She can outact Gong Li. When she shows up again, just wait to see the award I have to give her." He grabbed the mirror leg from Qilin's limp hand and resumed his search.

"Forget her," I told him. "The most important thing now is for us to check if the ceiling was blasted open. Come on." As I spoke I could hear a weird creaking sound as if something was slowly cracking apart.

"What the hell?" Fats shouted. "That sounds as though there's been a major breakthrough."

We looked up at the ceiling to find a huge gaping hole where seawater rushed through like a waterfall. The golden column that had held us earlier was split in two and had almost toppled over, which meant the ceiling was ready to fall as well.

"Relax," I told Fats, "this tomb is solid. Only an earthquake would topple it." And then the ground shook beneath our feet. Obviously the tomb was no longer airtight and water was rushing in from below as well as above us. If the floor collapsed before the ceiling fell, we would be in deep shit.

"What's happening?" Fats yelled.

"It's all right. This is normal. Get ready—the water will rush in soon and the pressure could knock us off our feet." My voice had hardly faded when there was a loud noise and the granite slab that we had used to block the tunnel opening shot away, carried by a huge flood of water. It was immediately followed by something else—the Forbidden Lady.

There was no time to worry about her. The water level was rising rapidly, carrying us up with it. There was still no trace of Ning.

We floated up and our heads soon were at the level of the ceiling. Suddenly Fats broke away and swam toward the walls.

"What are you doing?" I shouted as he brandished the mirror leg that he still held in his hand and dislodged one of the goose-egg pearls.

"Just wanted a little souvenir so I'll never forget the great time we've all had in this place," he gloated, and I wanted to drown him but the water was already up to my eyes. It was time to burst through the hole in the ceiling.

Fats was the weakest swimmer of the three of us so I motioned for him to leave first. He shook his head and yelled above the engulfing water, "I'm too fat. If I get stuck there, we'll all die."

I nodded and swam into the opening. It was wider at the bottom than it was at the top, and was surrounded by layers of sand which floated through the hole, creating a white mist. I could see nothing but paddled with all of my strength and floated up and out, just as I was about to suffocate. My head shot above the surface of the water and I gulped down deep breaths of air.

Fats and Qilin were soon beside me; Fats was choking and laughing at the same time. "Fuck me," he roared. "We're safe!"

I looked about and knew I had never seen anything so beautiful. The setting sun cast a reflection of crimson clouds on the surface of the sea and the sun itself was a dark red, beaming rays of pale yellow light that softened everything they touched. Even Fats looked serene and peaceful.

Then my legs seized with cramps and in a panic I looked for

our boat. There it was in a nearby reef, and at the sight of it I calmed down. A good meal, a good night's sleep—it sounded like heaven.

Fats, however, looked as though he had forgotten something. He dove back into the sea and I followed to bring him back to sanity. As he led me down, I saw Ning, stuck in the opening that we had just come through, struggling desperately to emerge.

Weird, I thought, Fats made it out with no problem, and Ning was perhaps an eighth of his size. How could she get stuck there?

As we approached, her face turned grey, bubbles issued from her open mouth, and the whites of her eyes bulged. Fats and I each grabbed one of her arms and pulled hard. A counterforce tugged her back into the hole but our strength prevailed. Like a cork from a bottle of champagne, Ning erupted toward us, and as I saw hair wrapped around her ear, I knew what the trouble was.

The hole was completely full of black hair. We knew the Forbidden Lady was on her way up and it was time for us to go. Ning was limp and weak but still breathing and we pulled her up onto the deck of the boat.

Water gushed from her mouth without stopping and her eyes rolled up into her head. "Captain!" I yelled. "This woman is dying!"

There was no reply. "Stay with her, Fats," I told him and went to the cabin. It was empty and there was no trace of anyone on board. I shouted several more times; nobody answered.

Fats came running to me and I said, "We're the only ones here."

"You're crazy," he scoffed. He walked through the boat and came back, shaking his head. "You're right. Where could they have gone?"

CHAPTER FORTY-FIVE
ENDING IT ALL

"Pirates," I yelled.

Fats nodded and said, "Of course. This is the South China Sea—it's full of Vietnamese, Malaysian, Japanese, even Thai. There are boats filled with illegal immigrants, drugs, weapons—but the weird thing is nothing's missing from this boat but the crew."

We walked into the galley and smelled the comforting fragrance of brewed tea leaves. A cup steamed on the table, still hot.

"Could they have been spirited onto the ghost ship?" Fats asked, taking a swig of the tea and smacking his lips.

I shrugged and walked into the wheelhouse. "Mayday. Unmanned boat," I called into the microphone of the radio. The only reply was an automated message: "Attention all boats! A typhoon warning has just been issued. Come to shore at once. Attention all boats! Please take shelter in the nearest harbor."

Fats and I exchanged glances. So much for being rescued. Fate was far from being our friend.

"Looks like we can't just sit here and wait or we'll all be thrown sky-high by the wind. Haul up the anchor and I'll head for shore," Fats ordered.

He lit a cigarette and turned a few valves and buttons, looking like quite the sailor. "Do you know what you're doing?" I asked. "This isn't like your Feng Shui bullshit, is it? If you fuck around here we'll all be fish food."

"You have no idea what I'm capable of, Young Wu. I can cook better than your mother and fly a plane too." Fats laughed. "I used to work on a fishing boat. Don't worry, just do as you're told."

He looked serious and glanced at a chart. "Reefs ahead here, I have to concentrate so don't bother me."

I went up to raise the anchor and then to check on Ning. Qilin was rubbing her hands to improve her circulation and although her color was better, her breathing was erratic.

"She's better," Qilin nodded as I looked at him questioningly.

In the galley, I found some packages of food and shared them with my companions. It wasn't so bad, I thought, we were dry and warm and had a bit of nourishment in our bellies. Sitting on the deck, leaning against the side of the wheelhouse, I fell asleep.

I awoke to an overcast sky and large waves. Looking in the wheelhouse I saw Fats snoring with Zhang Qilin at the helm. I collapsed back into exhaustion and woke to see Fats standing over me with a bowl of something that smelled wonderful.

"Pick up your chopsticks, Young Wu. It's time to eat." He smiled.

I took a bite and smiled. "Not bad, Fatso. Where did you learn to cook?"

"No mother, no wife. I had to learn. It's just soup—no

big deal."

"Thumbs-up, Fats. There aren't many people I admire but there's a lot for me to learn from you."

"Stop kissing my butt and eat before I gobble it all. And don't drool your spit in the bowl."

When he finished eating, Fats took over the helm again and started to sing "A Girl as Lovely as a Dazzling Pearl." He held something in his right hand and I blinked hard as I looked. It was the pearl he grabbed from the ceiling just before we escaped.

He handed it to me and said, "You're just idling around here. Help me come up with an estimate of how much money I can make from this."

I weighed it in my hand. "It's fake," I said.

Fats choked and turned bright red, staring at me in complete fury.

"Don't get so worked up," I consoled him. "It's not completely worthless; it's a fish-eye stone. You know what it means when people talk about passing off fish eyes for pearls? This is what they mean; it's pretty rare. You just have to see if you can find a buyer. I knew it was fake right away, the second I saw it. Think it over—so many goose-egg pearls in one ceiling. Who did you think Wang Canghai was? After all, there have only been about a dozen of these found in the tombs of Chinese royal families over the centuries."

The anger drained away from Fats's face as he yelled, "Next time just spit out what you have to say and don't make a person die of suspense. Now give me an estimate; what's this thing worth?"

"I've never seen anything like this but probably about

five hundred thousand yuan," I speculated.

"Forget it," Fats grumbled, "I risked my life for this damn thing—I'll turn it into a lamp before I give it away at that price."

"Just a second—I met a dealer with a fat-cat customer when I was in Jinan. I'll ask him about your fake pearl when I go back to check on Panzi—should be no problem to swap this for a mansion. Just stop talking about it now, will you?"

"I'm counting on you," Fats said. "I should have held my breath for a few more seconds and knocked down six more of these fish eyes. Then I could buy myself a little plane to zip around in, like a rich American."

His daydreaming had gone out of control and I turned away. He put the pearl back in his pocket and asked me, "We didn't find your Uncle Three. What are you going to do about that? I think you'll go nuts if you don't find the old bastard."

My plan was to go back to his house, ransack it, and see if I could figure out what my uncle was doing and who he really was, but I didn't want to discuss this with Fats. "What can I do? Go back to my little shop and forget about all this. I'm a businessman, not a grave robber."

Fats gave me a sharp glance and then laughed, but said nothing more. We were nearing the harbor at Yongxing Island and navigation took up all of his attention. The harbor was full of boats taking shelter from the coming typhoon and we were happy to get off our own vessel and feel land under our feet at last.

Fats immediately took Ning to a hospital and then we checked into a small hotel. We knew we would be stuck on this island until the storm was over and flights resumed to the mainland, so we made ourselves as comfortable as possible.

As we discussed our undersea adventure, we decided the tomb that almost killed us had to belong to Wang Canghai, although we were almost certain the strange corpse with a tail was not his body. And we had no idea who might have been buried in the Palace of Heaven on Mount Changbai but were sure it must have been a woman, since all of the mourners in the painting of the funeral procession were female.

Perhaps the biggest puzzle was the Bronze Fish with Snake Brows that was found both in the cavern of the blood zombies and in the undersea tomb, as well as the weird bells. What was the connection between these two places, or between the Ruler of Dead Soldiers and Wang Canghai, for that matter?

The most horrible theory was advanced by Qilin, who pointed out to us that there were unexplored spaces in the tomb we just left that probably had additional chambers. It was customary for important people to place rare birds and animals in secret rooms that were then walled off. This is where the monsters that almost destroyed us had probably been kept.

"Holy shit," I said in disgust. "You mean that the sea monkey and the Forbidden Lady had been captured as pets for Wang Canghai's amusement and then buried alive?"

Qilin nodded. "He wouldn't have been the first to do that. Hideous creatures and rare animals have been found in a few imperial tombs from the Shang and

45. ENDING IT ALL

Zhou dynasties as well as in the mausoleum of the First Emperor, Qin Shi Huang. It was considered normal to do that in ancient times."

As the typhoon raged, we slowly regained our strength and energy. Fats was relieved to see that the white feathers on his back were gone and I wondered if it could have been because of my spit, while he often chattered about buying some of my miraculous aftershave.

I didn't really care about what became of the feathers or about anything else. My physical energy had returned but my mind was still apathetic and listless. To amuse myself, I tried to find out more about Qilin but he lay on his bed, staring at the ceiling and acting as though Fats and I didn't exist. Bored, I went down to the lobby of the hotel where there was a public computer and I was happy to find the typhoon hadn't destroyed the Internet connection.

Still wondering about Zhang Qilin, I typed in his name and pressed "search." It was hopeless; his name was too common and a hundred entries popped up. I clicked on one or two but found nothing.

Feeling annoyed, I typed in the name Wu Sansheng and found only one result, a missing person's notice. Clicking on it, I brought up a photo of a group of people, among them Wen-Jin and Zhang Qilin. It was a picture of the first group that had disappeared in the undersea tomb—the long-lost students—and standing in the middle of them was my Uncle Three.

I quickly scanned the notice. It listed the names of the people who had been lost twenty years ago, and at the end of the list was a short sentence. I read it and my mouth went dry. It said, "The fish is at my place."

VOL
3

Coming Next:

"The fish is at my place."

What fish? Could this be the third Bronze Fish with Snake Brows?

The carving in the undersea tomb showed three of these fish all connected, head to tail. I had two of them, but there ought to be one more. Did this sentence mean someone else had the third fish?

I scrolled through the notice once more and saw it had been posted two years ago. There was no contact information for the person who had put it on the Internet, nor could I find any related links to the post. Whoever had posted this had a photo of Uncle Three's group—and knew about the fish. Who could this be?

When the storm cleared, we were more than ready to leave the island, but first we went to the hospital to check on Ning. She was gone, the doctor told us, taken away by a group of foreigners a few days before.

"God damn it," Fats grumbled. "She got away again."

"It's a good thing. What were we going to do with her? We couldn't torture her to make her tell us who she worked for or what she knew about the tomb," I said. "Now she's the foreigners' problem, not ours. She's never been anything but a big pain in the ass—I'm glad she's gone."

Nevertheless, it was plain that the company that had asked us to find their missing boat had more at stake than that. What had they really been searching for? Did my uncle know? Had he been working with them? Where was he now? When would the answers to these questions emerge from the South China Sea near Xisha?

TO BE CONTINUED...

Note from the Author

Back in the days when there was no television or internet and I was still a poor kid, telling stories to other children was my greatest pleasure. My friends thought my stories were a lot of fun, and I decided that someday I would become the best of storytellers.

I wrote a lot of stories trying to make that dream come true, but most of them I put away, unfinished. I completely gave up my dream of being a writer, and like many people, I sat waiting for destiny to tap me on the shoulder.

Although I gave up my dream of being a writer, luckily the dream did not give up on me. When I was 26 years old, my uncle, a merchant who sold Chinese antiques, gave me his journal that was full of short notes he had written over the years. Although fragmentary information can often be quite boring, my uncle's writing inspired me to go back to my abandoned dream. A book about a family of grave robbers began to take shape, a suspenseful novel.... I started to write again....

This is my first story, my first book that became successful beyond all expectations, a best-seller that made me rich. I have no idea how this happened, nor does anybody else; this is probably the biggest mystery of The Grave Robbers' Chronicles. Perhaps as you read the many volumes of this chronicle, you will find out why it has become so popular. I hope you enjoy the adventures you'll encounter with Uncle Three, his nephew and their companions as they roam through a world of zombies, vampires, and corpse-eaters.

Thanks to Albert Wen, Michelle Wong, Janet Brown, Kathy Mok and all my friends who helped publish the English edition of The Grave Robbers' Chronicles.

Xu Lei was born in 1982 and graduated from Renmin University of China in 2004. He has held numerous jobs, working as a graphic designer, a computer programmer, and a supplier to the U.S. gaming industry. He is now the owner of an international trading company and lives in Hangzhou, China with his wife and son. Writing isn't his day job, but it is where his heart lies.